# CANDY KISSES
*A Sweet Treat Valentine's Novella*

# BERNADETTE MARIE

This is a fictional work. The names, characters, incidents, places, and locations are solely the concepts and products of the author's imagination or are used to create a fictitious story and should not be construed as real.

**5 PRINCE PUBLISHING AND BOOKS, LLC**
PO Box 16507
Denver, CO 80216
www.5PrinceBooks.com
www.BernadetteMarie.com

ISBN 13: 978-1-63112-028-2 ISBN 10: 163112028X

Second Edition/Second Printing February 2014 Printed U.S.A.

5 PRINCE PUBLISHING AND BOOKS, LLC.

For Stan
On Valentine's Day and Forever and a day!

# ACKNOWLEDGMENTS

To Antoinette and Connie who took a lot of effort to make this possible. To all of the beta readers at 5 Prince Publishing who seize the opportunity to read my work before anyone else has the opportunity to do so, thank you. To my parents and my children who support me in every endeavor. To my husband who loves me unconditionally, even when I don't help pay the bills. And last but not least to Susan. Without your guidance I would never have been able to have accomplished so much in such a little amount of time. Your graciousness with your talents has brought me to where I am today. I am blessed that fate put us on the path it did and that you will forever remain more than just an editor or mentor. You will always be my friend.

# ACKNOWLEDGMENTS

# CHAPTER ONE

Three hundred more truffles needed to be rolled and Tabitha's hands had long gone numb. On any other day she'd take the time to stretch her fingers or even run them under warm water to relieve the cramping. But it was February and that meant no stopping until the fifteenth. It was also spontaneous wedding season where people jumped at the thought of marriage and that always made for a lot more work.

She blew a loose strand of hair from her eyes and kept making perfectly round balls from the batter before setting them on the lined tray to her side. She couldn't remember a year when she'd had as many wedding chocolates to make. Her biggest client Claire Banks, an esteemed wedding planner, must have booked every day in February with a wedding or party. And she had chosen Tabitha Chocolates to tempt the guests at every table.

It was work that Tabitha lived for, but added to her already heavy workload before Valentine's Day, she was feeling a bit pinched for time and her mood was sinking fast.

"Okay, it's done." Brie darted into the prep area of Tabitha's small Cherry Creek store, waving a work order. "We just picked up the Johnson-Carr wedding."

Tabitha squished the dough ball in her hand. "How are we going to get this all done?

We might need to start saying no," she grumbled as she rolled yet another truffle through the cocoa and then set it on the tray to dry.

"Hey listen, Ms. Valentine and Wedding-Scrooge, I've been planning a tropical vacation with grass huts and fruity drinks with umbrellas. We need all the weddings we can get so I can make the big bucks and get out of this icebox for a while." Brie hung the order on a clipboard on the order wall.

Tabitha scowled as she scooped out a dozen more truffles to be rolled through the coating and set them on the tray. "Scrooge, huh?"

"You work too hard. You forget what it's like to have men fall at your feet at least one day a year."

"Yet you and my mother seem to think it should happen all the time. I mean, how many times can the woman get engaged and married on Valentine's Day? Doesn't it take away the special meaning?"

"Maybe she does it just to piss you off." Brie grinned, and Tabitha wondered if her and her mother didn't just plan to make her crazy on purpose.

Tabitha shook her head as Brie went back to answering the phone at the front counter. Sometimes your best friends shouldn't be the people you hire.

She blew out a breath and thought of the upcoming holiday. She couldn't help but be cynical in February. People turned starry-eyed and lovesick all because of a greeting card holiday. She, for one, knew better than to believe in such fanciful dreams.

Her own mother had fallen head over heels in love on Valentine's Day. Who thinks that meeting the man of your dreams is possible when selling flowers on the street corner? And how asinine is it to run off with a man whose tongue dripped satin words? Marriage after four days of shacking up in a hotel room did not make for a lifetime of happy memories, Tabitha thought as she dusted her hands off on her apron. She hopped down from the stool, on which she'd been perched for hours, and sought out a cup of coffee.

As she washed the cocoa from her hands, she gave thought to the phrase "love at first sight." The idea was ridiculous, but people fell for it all the time. And there she was, making money off of their sentimental dreams.

She opened the cupboard and pulled down her favorite, green, oversized mug. She poured strong, black coffee inside and rested against the counter. She wasn't sure why she was worried about who fell in love. It paid her bills, and it appeared that love would soon send Brie on a tropical vacation.

By late afternoon, Tabitha had rolled thousands of truffles. She had rolled some in cocoa and others in milk chocolate. Another batch was set aside for a variety of white and dark chocolate. Prepping strawberries for tomorrow's dipping would keep her busy for the rest of the night.

Brie poked her head into the workroom. "I locked up and am going to head out. I have a date." She wiggled her eyebrows and Tabitha shook her head. When did the girl not have a date? "Would you mind cleaning out the display?"

"Of course." Tabitha laid a long stem strawberry out on a tray to dry.

"I closed out the register." Brie pulled her coat from the rack and slipped it on.

"Who are you going out with?"

"Video store guy. He is so fine that I think I've fallen in love."

Tabitha shook her head. Did this new love know Brie had fallen in love already three other times since New Year's Eve?

With Brie gone, Tabitha turned on the radio to fill the silence. She'd laid out the strawberries and set them on the rack, then pushed it into the cooler.

The storefront was dark and the sign had been turned to closed. Tabitha began the process of removing the few unsold chocolates from the display and boxing them to sell on the shelves the next day. It was rare that she discarded any chocolate. Her business had been voted one of the best stores in both Cherry Creek and Denver, and her chocolate was ordered online all over the world. She laughed to herself when she thought about how *sweet* business had been for her.

Tabitha bent over and pulled a tray from the case. When she stood, she saw the face of a man, his gloved hands cupped around his eyes, looking into the store. She nearly dropped the tray of petit fours to the ground. When he'd seen her, he'd stepped back and waved.

Her heart beat at an uncomfortable pace. This was one of those times she wished she'd taken her mother's advice and planted a gun under the counter. The idea was as stupid as the grin on the man's lips that told her he wasn't dangerous. Or, at least, she hoped so.

She set down the tray and walked to the door, her hands shaking from the startle he'd given her. The man stepped back, still grinning widely as Tabitha pointed to the CLOSED sign.

"Please." She could hear him plead through the door.

It wasn't like her to open the door to a stranger, but this one had a familiar look to him, though she was sure she'd never seen him before. She looked around the streets and people still walked between the stores. If she had to scream, someone would likely hear her.

She unlocked the door and opened it slightly, keeping her foot blocked behind it. "We're closed."

"I know. I'm so sorry. I just flew in from a convention in New York, my flight was late, and the bus to the parking lot was—"

"Sir," she cut him off, holding her hand up. "You'll have to come back tomorrow."

"Listen, I'll pay double if you'll help me out. It's my mother's birthday and I've already missed the party. If I don't walk through the door with a box of Tabitha Chocolates and bat my big, brown eyes at her, she'll have my head."

She considered him for a moment. "Batting your eyes won't work on its own?" The trick seemed to be working on her.

"I don't think so. Not this time."

His short, brown hair had tunnels where his fingers must have raked through dozens of times. Dark circles shadowed under his eyes, which when fully alert she assumed would burn into a woman with their dark brown warmth. The collar of his shirt was open and his tie hung loosely around his neck. The long, wool coat, which should have kept him nice and warm in the bitter cold of Denver's winter, gaped open across his chest.

Against her better judgment, Tabitha moved her foot from behind the door and let him into the store.

She walked around the counter quickly to put space between them. "I'm afraid I don't have much of a selection. A week before Valentine's Day we're usually sold out of the favorites."

The man stopped and looked at the bare shelves in the display as he pulled his hands from his gloves. "You probably know my mother. She comes in often enough. Maybe you could help me throw together something."

"Who is your mother?"

"Claire Banks."

"Your mother is Claire Banks?" The image of his mother crossed her mind. Looking at the handsome man across from her, she found it hard to believe that Claire's son was such a head turner.

"You do know her."

"Of course I know her." Half of her order board had the woman's name on it, thankfully. "I mean no disrespect, but really, do you think a box of chocolates is what she needs for her birthday?" She hated how it sounded the moment it came out. But when the corners of his mouth turned up into a smile, which sent an alarming sizzle through her, she realized she hadn't offended him.

He leaned his arms on the top of the case. "My father tried to buy her flowers once. She said she didn't get any joy out of looking at pretty things. She'd rather eat pretty things. I prefer to appease her and think of her health later."

A giggle grew in her chest and she kept it forced down. This man was keeping her at work even later than she'd anticipated. She just wanted his money and wanted him out. "She enjoys the petit fours quite a bit. I could probably spare some of the truffles I dipped a few hours ago, but I won't have the strawberries until the morning."

"Dear Lord, how much time does she spend in here?"

"Client confidentiality." She smiled and it almost hurt, which made her realize she'd been doing her fair share of scowling lately. Februarys were usually for profit and hard work, not for smiling at handsome men.

"You have the most beautiful eyes."

The comment had her swallowing back the smile. Her spine stiffened. "I beg your pardon."

"Really. They're the color of milk chocolate with swirls of caramel. It's no wonder you're so good at being a chocolatier. It must run through your blood."

"This isn't going to get you a price discount or strawberries in that box."

That smile crossed his lips again. "Oh, I didn't mean any disrespect." Humor filled his voice. "I appreciate fine art the way my mother appreciates fine chocolates. Your eyes, like your chocolates, are beautiful. I'm sorry that you mind that I told you that."

"I don't mind." She turned and pulled a white pastry box from the shelf behind her. Inside it, she adjusted the paper doily. "I'm just not comfortable with strangers looking at me the way you do."

"Well then, I suppose we should fix that." He reached his hand over the counter. "Preston

Banks. Son of Claire Banks, the distinguished wedding planner."

Hesitantly, she shook his hand. "Tabitha Knight, the wedding planner's choice for her chocolates. Privately and professionally."

His eyes widened. "You're Tabitha? As in Tabitha Chocolates? As in owner of the store?"

She pulled her hand from his, uncomfortable with his reaction. "You seem surprised."

"Well, I wouldn't have pictured you as the entrepreneur type."

"You wouldn't?"

"I mean ..." He raked his fingers through his hair, deepening the channels where his fingers had traveled before. "What I meant to say was that I expected the name to only be a name. How many young and attractive women have their handmade products in some of the most exclusive shops and on the trays at the most elegant weddings?"

She swallowed back the urge to gasp at the attractive comment. She was out of her element. These were the kind of comments Brie usually received. "You seem to know my work well."

"Claire Banks is my mother, remember?"

Tabitha gave into her smile again. "She has been a substantial help to my business. I do tend to be on her list of people to call when she's planning a wedding."

"Then with Valentine's Day around the corner you must be extremely busy."

"You have no idea." And, she thought, if he'd only finish his purchase she could get back to work on those orders his mother had placed for clients.

"That's why I cut my trip short and I'm headed to her place. Not only is it her birthday, but this year it seems she's bitten off more than she can chew. She's booked one too many weddings this year, and now the entire family is in charge of seeing they all go off without a hitch."

"Awfully nice that you could help her out."

Tabitha began filling the box with items she knew Claire Banks would enjoy.

Preston looked around. "How did you get into this?"

"Chocolate?" He let out an agreeable hum and she shrugged. "It was something I always loved. I fell in love with my Tabitha Hobby Oven and making those little cakes."

"Were you one of those girls who wouldn't share? My sisters never would share Easy-Bake cakes with me."

Tabitha added a few more candies to the box. "I made one of my mother's first wedding cakes in my oven. Soon it turned into cookies and decorating the tops. Then I learned the fine art of a double boiler and a chocolatier was born." She counted out the items in the box silently. "And with my mother's affection for getting married every few years, it seemed like a good hobby to acquire."

"And how many times has she been married?" The humor in his eyes raked on her nerves when he asked.

"On Valentine's Day, it will be her fifth."

"Fifth?" His voice rose in pitch.

Tabitha hated reactions like that, but that's what she got for opening her big mouth. She shook her head in disgust as she added a few more truffles to the box. He was irritating her, and he was going to pay for it as the box was getting heavier.

He shook his head. "All I can say is wow. Is she using my mother to plan her wedding?"

"If I were only that lucky. No, as if I weren't busy enough, she's somehow designated me as her bridal planner." Tabitha added the last petit fours from the tray she'd taken from the display and closed the box.

"Where do you find time if this is your busy season?"

"A question I've asked myself." She laid the box atop the display. "This is sixty dollars' worth of Tabitha Chocolates. Do you want me to dig up more, or do you think she'll be fine with this?"

"I think she'll be delighted." He handed her a fifty and a twenty, not once blinking at the price. Perhaps she should have added quite a bit more.

"I'll be back. I've closed the drawer so I have to get you change." She turned to walk to her office.

"No," he said, and she stopped. "Consider it my thank you for opening the door."

"I appreciate it, but that's not necessary."

"I insist."

At that, she turned and pulled a ribbon from a spool that hung on the wall. Carefully she lifted the box and tied the ribbon around it.

Preston watched her intently and lifted his eyes to hers when she finished with the bow. "Are you busy tomorrow night?"

"I'm sorry. What?" Her tone carried her impatience. She just wanted to get back to work so she could finally get home.

"I'd love to take you to dinner."

She adjusted the bow atop the box and added a gold foiled sticker with the name of the bakery. "Mr. Banks, thank you, but ..."

"Preston," he reminded her with a smile. It did its job in calming her, but she wasn't comfortable with a stranger asking her out. She was in unfamiliar territory.

"Preston. I don't go out with men I've only just met."

"Why?"

"Why? It's that simple. I don't know you."

"No, but you could if you have dinner with me. Unless you're married." His brows drew together and the creases around his lips deepened. "I didn't think about that."

"I'm not married."

"Great," he said. "I'll stop by here after you close. If you're not done, I'd be happy to help you."

"You talk fast." She held her hands up as if to stop him. "Do you sell used cars?"

"No, only the finest BMWs and Jags." He smiled when she scowled. "I don't really have to do a lot of talking. The cars sell themselves. But if I keep talking the buyer can't walk away from the sale."

"I'm walking away."

"No, you're not. You're going to let me take you to dinner tomorrow because now you're intrigued. And because my mother is not only one of your biggest customers with her business, she's a great fan of yours as well." He reached over the counter and grabbed her hand. He lifted it to his lips and brushed her knuckles with a kiss. "Tabitha, it certainly was my pleasure to meet you. Thank you for helping me out. I'll see you tomorrow." He picked up his box and walked out the door.

Tabitha stood still, rendered speechless by the man who had waltzed in and out of her store. Apparently she was having dinner with the man. Had she said yes?

She wouldn't go. No one talked her into things like that. The last thing she needed in February was some man taking her to dinner. She was much too busy.

As she folded the money he'd handed her and shoved it into her pocket, she thought of Preston Banks and his playful smile. He was right. She was definitely intrigued.

# CHAPTER TWO

One day closer to Valentine's Day and Tabitha watched as Brie flirted with the man at the counter. She laughed at his jokes, touched his hand, and made the motion of swinging her hair back over her shoulder even though it was in a ponytail high on her head. Tabitha considered the whole ritual disgusting, but he'd bought a box of thirty-dollar chocolates for his girlfriend and two more matching boxes for his mother and grandmother.

When the man walked out of the store, Brie whistled as she walked past Tabitha and rearranged the display in the case.

Tabitha shook her head. "Doesn't it bother you to use your female charm to sell things?"

"He came in here wanting a four pack of truffles. A four pack," she emphasized with her fingers held up. "He walked out spending ninety. Do you really see a problem?"

She winced. "I see a problem with the whole holiday and the whole month of February. But as long as people like you roam the streets thinking that love lurks around the corner, I'll make my car payment and my mortgage nicely for the next year until I have to watch you all do it again."

"I've decided we should find you a florist that hates February, weddings, and Mother's Day too. I imagine the two of you would fall madly in love." Brie leaned against the counter and crossed her arms over her chest. "Just think, you could make all the money off those of us who believe in romance, love at first sight, and till death do us part. And the two of you could sit around your own kitchen table and just shake your heads at us as we spend money in your stores." She raised her hands in the air with her palms up. "It would be a match made in heaven, or hell – wherever it is you live in that head of yours. The chocolatier that doesn't believe in Valentine's Day and love."

"You're mean," Tabitha snarled at her best friend, who sadly knew her much too well.

"I'm realistic. Love is wonderful."

"Love is overrated." Tabitha watched the woman who stood at her window waving a gloved hand. "And this is why I think love is overrated."

The woman opened the door and shut it quickly. "Oh, it is freezing out there." She smiled her million dollar smile at Tabitha and beelined around the counter. "There is my beautiful daughter."

Her mother gave her a noisy kiss on the cheek and stood with her gloved hands cupping Tabitha's face. "You're working too hard." She studied her intently. "You need some time off."

"Mom, I don't have time for time off." She took her mother's hands from her face and forced a smile. "This is the season where I make most of my money. Add that silly day in

May where we worship our mothers and my year is paid for."

"You do worship me." Her mother turned to Brie before Tabitha rolled her eyes and shook her head. "She's mad because she's doing the chocolates for my wedding."

"That's a tossup, Corrine," Brie interjected. "She's mad because she doesn't think I should flirt with customers to make them spend three times what they came in to spend."

"Foolish," her mother laughed as she took off her gloves and her heavy, suede coat. She draped it over her arm and then, with her perfectly manicured fingers, adjusted the pearls which hung from her wrist. Her nail polish was red, and it had been as far back as Tabitha could remember.

"It won't stop me either," Brie added. "If they want to open their wallets while I giggle at their lame jokes, then I am happy to oblige."

"You two are horrible." Tabitha walked to the back of the store and pulled out a tray of long stem strawberries from the drying rack.

Her mother followed her. She set her coat on the stool by the door and pulled up another to the table where Tabitha worked. She sat down and crossed her legs. Her foot, in its fashionable yet very unpractical shoe, bounced to the beat on the radio. "Peter and I registered yesterday. It was very exciting."

"What could you possibly have registered for?"

"Don't belittle my wedding," she said, looking over her manicure. "Peter is the best, isn't he?"

Tabitha didn't wish to get into the war of words that were brewing in her head. She agreed with a nod and let it go.

"Well, the reason I wanted to stop by was to tell you to double our order. We downsized the cake so we could show you off more."

Tabitha lifted her head and stared at her mother. "Are you kidding me? Mom, your wedding is in two weeks. I have five other weddings and this silly holiday that makes all of you lovesick people crazy. I can't fit in time to double that order."

"You'll do it for me," she said grinning.

Tabitha was sure her mother's common sense had never developed. But one thing was true. She'd do it for her mother and she hated herself for it.

"Fine. I'll do it. But if Claire Banks needs more, I'll do her weddings first. She pays me full price."

"Is it always the money?"

She wanted to tell her it was the principle but, as her mother was still glassy eyed thinking of her wedding, she just couldn't do it.

Brie poked her head through the doorway. "Um, Tab, you have a visitor." She bit her lip, but the edges of her mouth turned up into smile.

"Who?"

"A gentleman who says he's come to take you to dinner."

"What?" Tabitha wiped her hands on her apron and noticed the expression of joy that crossed her mother's face.

She walked to the front of the store and there stood Preston Banks. He was dressed casually in jeans and dark leather jacket. Handsome was the first thing Tabitha thought as she watched him give her a nervous smile.

Her mother gave her a slight shove toward him and she turned to scowl, but she was sure her mother never noticed. She was starry-eyed, looking at Preston as though he were Prince Charming and came baring a golden slipper.

He took a step toward her. "I know I'm really early, but I was afraid if I waited you'd lock up and leave without me."

Truth was she'd forgotten about telling him she'd go to dinner because she'd been so busy with orders. No, she suddenly remembered, he'd tricked her into a dinner date. Well, now she was very glad he was there so she could tell him that under no circumstances was she going to go out with him. He was a total stranger. She didn't go out with men she didn't know.

Her mother shoved past her. "Oh, and here I'm keeping her from getting ready." She shot her hand out toward Preston. "I'm Tabby's mother, Corinne."

Tabitha felt her stomach churn. Perhaps she'd become violently ill and die.

Preston gave a gracious nod as he shook Corinne's hand. "I see where your daughter gets her lovely looks."

"You are a prize." A laugh poured from her mother.

"Well, Tab, why don't you introduce me to your new *boyfriend*." Brie walked around the counter and joined her mother by Preston's side.

Now not only did she feel her stomach twisting, she could feel the blood drain from her face. For a moment, she wasn't sure if the better idea was to introduce them and die, or leave with the man just to escape the goofy looks from the two women who didn't understand reality.

"Preston, this is Brie. My least favorite friend at the moment." She narrowed her eyes on her as Brie brushed her aside and shook Preston's hand.

"She didn't mention she had a date." The look on Brie's face was the same as when she'd flirted her way to the bigger sale.

"Didn't she?"

Preston had turned to look at her and was gazing at her. Not looking, but gazing. She'd seen that look on the men that Brie conned out of bigger sales, but they didn't look at her that way.

Now her mouth dried and her stomach was still very uncomfortable.

Preston reached for her hand and gave it a gentle squeeze. "I can just make myself comfortable in the corner until you're ready."

"She's ready," Brie and her mother answered in unison.

"We'll close up," Brie committed before Tabitha could protest. "I'll get your things."

Within moments, her mother had helped her out of her apron, and Brie had managed to slide her into her coat and tighten the ponytail at the base of her neck while Preston looked on smiling.

"It looks like you're all ready to go. It was a pleasure to meet you both." Preston took Tabitha's arm and started toward the door. "I won't keep her out too late."

Tabitha let Preston guide her to his car with his hand on her elbow. Aside from the fact that the sidewalk was slick, she supposed he was being a gentleman.

She turned back to see her mother and Brie watching from the window. She couldn't help but wonder where she'd lost her spine. Somehow, she'd been kicked out of her own business and was going to spend the evening with a man she didn't know. This would have been a typical night for Brie, or her mother, but certainly was a first for her.

There was some comfort in that she knew his mother. But Claire Banks was only a client, not a close and personal friend. For all Tabitha knew, the entire Banks family could be a group of raving lunatics. The thought humored her. Okay, she had to be honest with herself. They didn't seem like lunatics at all. Just a nice, well-rounded family.

Preston opened the car door for her, and she climbed into the passenger seat of the BMW as he skirted around the front of the car and then climbed in next to her. The cold air blew through as he shut the door to block it out. "I would have had it all warmed up for you, but I didn't know we'd be leaving so soon." He started the engine and the heater kicked on.

"I'm sorry about the two of them. Though loving, they are crazy." She could still see them, their faces pressed against the glass of the door, grinning from ear to ear.

"I found them endearing." He pulled away from the curb and headed out of town. "I thought we'd head up to Morrison. I know a wonderful, little sushi place."

He'd turned to her and she assumed he was waiting to see her reaction, whether she would turn up her nose or would smile. She kept her face as still as she could.

He looked back at the road. "You don't like sushi?"

"I like it fine, but Morrison is a little further than I figured we'd go." Then again, maybe he was a lunatic. Didn't they take women up into the hills? She shook away the thought. This was why she didn't date men she didn't already know.

He didn't apologize or offer to turn back. "I won't hurt you. I promise."

She let out a loud huff of breath. "I didn't plan on giving you a chance."

When he laughed at her, she couldn't help but find his laughter sexy. It was low and husky. She should have felt offended that he was laughing, but she didn't feel as though it was directed at her.

He rested his hand on the gearshift knob. "You don't appear to be the kind of woman who would let a man hurt her."

"You're right."

Preston glanced casually at her. "I think I would surprise you with what I already know."

Tabitha narrowed her stare on him. "I would guess you spoke to your mother?"

"Of course. She wants me to tell you she loved the selection you picked for her, by the way, and that she'll also be calling you with a small wedding she picked up yesterday. It's only a thirty person, private wedding, but she thought she'd give you a heads up."

Tabitha let out a sigh when she thought about adding one more wedding, but, then again, it was one more payment on her car.

He focused back on the road. "Anyway, I told her I'd met you and asked you to dinner. She's thrilled."

"Is she? I still won't give you a discount."

He laughed again, and she wasn't comfortable with what it did to her. She should be infuriated that he'd somehow gotten her in his car and was laughing at her, but she couldn't be. There was a relaxed quality about Preston Banks. It was something Tabitha had never felt around a man. When he laughed, he laughed easily. When he smiled, it was genuine. And though he talked in circles to get what he wanted, he was pleasant.

As they drove west toward the mountains that gave Colorado its identity, with the jagged peaks of Red Rocks glowing from the setting sun, he told her of his life in luxury car sales.

Tabitha searched her mind for small talk that would move away from how busy she was and how his mother kept adding to her workload. "How did you get into selling cars?"

"I'll be honest. It wasn't a career I thought I'd choose. But right out of college my roommate tells me his dad needs some help for the summer at his car lot. I'm thinking one of those lots where the hoods are tied down and they don't let you see the flaws, they just sell you the car." She nodded. She'd known a few places like that. He focused on changing lanes near the Morrison exit and eased off the highway. "So I show up the first day and, of course, I was stunned when it was a legit dealership which, at the time, sold Fords."

"So you didn't start in luxury?"

"I know everything there is about the Ford line." He smiled brilliantly. "They began to expand. Eventually they opened a BMW location and he sent me off to head it up."

"Head it up?" She turned to him. "You run it?"

"General Manager. It's my show."

She turned back. "Impressive." He certainly knew how to manage people. The proof was her sitting in his car.

It should have been a conversation that bored her to sleep. But he had a soothing voice, and genuine enthusiasm for what he did, and she found herself interested.

Preston pulled into the lot outside a small building, set back from the main street lined with small restaurants, bars, and gift shops. It was a rustic cabin and not what Tabitha had in mind when he'd said sushi.

He parked the car, climbed out, hurried to the other side, and opened her door. He reached for her hand and helped her out. The cold that hit her was different from that in the city. The air was crisper and still. The large hills blocked the wind from blowing through them.

When he took her hand and interlaced their fingers, she felt a surge of heat flash through her in sharp contrast to the cold that surrounded them. For a moment she couldn't move. She could only take in the sight of him.

His eyes and hair grew darker in the shadows cast by the sunset. Tabitha hadn't had time to appreciate the strong lines of his face. He was taller than she'd remembered when he'd stood on the other side of her display, and she wondered if he'd worn that same scent which carried on the February breeze and penetrated her senses, sending tingles over her skin.

Preston reached for her other hand and linked their fingers as he looked down at her. "You are a beautiful woman, Tabitha. I'm so happy you weren't just a name of a chocolate company."

He lifted her hand to his lips and gently brushed his lips over her knuckles before placing a soft kiss in the palm of her hand. She swallowed back the thrill it sent through her.

"Preston, please don't get the wrong idea about tonight. It's just dinner."

"That's all I asked for, if I remember correctly."

Tabitha nodded. Perhaps he did understand the situation.

Because being around Preston Banks seemed to bring calm to her that she'd never felt, she'd tasted dishes she never would have tried. When it came to sushi, she was fine with the cooked items or the vegetarian rolls.

Preston, however, enjoyed the more exotic. She quickly found she didn't enjoy octopus, but she could say she'd sampled it.

"Sushi anywhere is good. But, I'll be honest, sushi in a landlocked state doesn't hold a candle to the freshness of somewhere by the ocean." He dipped a piece of tuna into his soy sauce and then ate the entire piece with his cheeks puffing out because his mouth was full.

"Where have you gone with the best sushi?"

Preston thought for a moment while he drank his hot tea. "There is a little place in Manhattan that is my favorite. I had it just last week when I was there. But there is a place in Maui." He closed his eyes and smiled. "The tuna is unlike anything I've ever had." He sighed and opened his eyes.

Maui. It was funny that the mere mention of the tropical spot had her thinking that he had probably vacationed with a woman there and the focus wasn't on the sushi and tuna at all. The thought stuck in her chest and she fought to make it go away.

Who cared if Preston Banks had gone away on some secluded vacation with some woman? Why should she be jealous? She didn't even know the man. The pain it caused was uncomfortable, and it made her hate the whole dating process even more.

The air was frigid when they left the restaurant, but, thanks to technology, Preston had started the car from inside and when Tabitha slid onto the warm leather seat she was at ease.

"Thank you for dinner. I had a wonderful time."

"Thank you for coming with me." He backed out of the parking lot and headed back to the highway. "I'm sorry again for picking you up so early. I know I have a tendency to talk people into things, and I wouldn't have blamed you if you hadn't been there."

"I wouldn't have been." She was honest. "Preston," she turned her head to catch his eyes, darkened by the night. "I don't believe in all of this. I think it's fair to let you know."

"In what?" His voice was smooth.

"I don't believe in relationships or soul mates. I don't believe in Valentine's Day or love at first sight. It's not real."

Preston nodded as he merged with the traffic on the highway. "My mother would be very disappointed to hear her favorite chocolatier say such things. You do know she's booked weddings on the fact that she uses you exclusively."

"I didn't know that."

"Yep, and she's a fool for love." He tilted his head toward her, and she assumed he meant Claire was already planning a future for her and Preston.

Tabitha huffed out a laugh. "Our mothers are quite a pair." She didn't let it bother her.

Preston didn't seem like the kind of man who would press the issue.

For a moment, she enjoyed the drive with the mountains to her left and the lights of the city on her right. It was obvious he was taking the long way back to her store, but she didn't mention it. She was enjoying the drive. She was enjoying him.

"Do you believe in all of it?" she asked, breaking the silence between them.

"All of what?"

"Valentine's Day. Love at first sight. Forever?"

Preston reached for her hand and linked their fingers again. "If I find the right woman, I think all of that would be important."

She swallowed hard. "I've seen it fall apart too often. I mean, my mother is getting married for the fifth time. Four failed marriages and multiple other relationships that didn't last don't lead me to believe in the longevity of love."

Preston shifted his eyes to her and then back to the road. "You wouldn't give it a try?"

"No."

He shrugged. "That's too bad."

She sat back in her seat. "I only agreed to dinner, remember?"

"And I didn't ask for more, did I?" His voice was calm where hers hadn't been.

Now she felt foolish.

The sky was dark and the stars were bright against the black sky. It was beautiful. She often forgot, living in the lights of the city, what beauty there was just beyond her front door.

Preston pulled off the highway and parked in a lot at the edge of the Hog Back, a geological site she remembered visiting as a child on field trips. In the daylight, you could see the many colors of the rock formations from where they had cut through to build the highway, which now separated the two sides.

He turned off the engine and sat for a moment in the silence. "I know it's frigid, but what do you say we take a little walk and look out at the city?"

She couldn't help but feel the buzz of excitement brewing in her, which surprised her after she'd shot down all the wonderful things about relationships.

There was no way to suppress the fact that she was enjoying herself and hadn't wanted the night to end. It came as quite a surprise to her since she hadn't wanted to have dinner with him at all.

They made the small climb up the path to the end of the trail and looked out over the merging highways that took their bends around the rising hills. Denver splayed out in front of them in brilliant colors.

Tabitha shivered as a breeze blew through. Preston moved in next to her. He placed his hands on her arms and instinctively she settled against him.

She let herself take a moment and enjoy the warmth of him standing so close to her. His firm body pressed against her, his hands on her arms, and his warm breath on her cheek. "This is amazing. I've never been up here at night to see the lights. It's the perfect spot for everything. You have the city, the rocks, the mountains, and the traffic moving people everywhere."

"I didn't notice."

She turned her head to find his dark eyes gazing down at her. He took the band which held her hair back and pulled it free, letting her hair fall over her shoulders.

"I've wondered what that would look like," he said as he ran his hand over the length of her hair. "I told you your eyes looked like milk chocolate, but in the shadows your hair is like black satin." Tabitha swallowed hard and tried to look away, but his eyes locked onto hers. He touched her cheek and his hand was still warm. "You're freezing out here," he said as he stroked her cheek with his thumb.

She'd forgotten she was cold and that her face was numb. In fact, she couldn't remember ever being in a man's presence when she'd felt a fire burn through her as she did with Preston standing before her.

He combed his fingers through her hair once more. "I should get you home. I know you have a lot of work to do tomorrow, and it would be rude of me to keep you out too late."

He hesitated and Tabitha moved her gaze to his lips. The traffic below them seemed to silence as she could only hear her heart beating in her ears. She wanted him to kiss her. The desire to have him press his lips to her shivering ones was enough to drive her mad. Never, in all her life, had she wished someone would make such a move.

Every encounter with a man she'd ever had was coldly calculated. This was spontaneous.

Then it hit her like the frigid air. She stepped back from him and the bitter cold froze her to the bone. She'd been on the verge of moving in and kissing him herself. She'd wished he'd hold her, touch her, kiss her, and God knows what else. Not even thirty hours had passed since she'd met him. This is where it began. This was the moment women turned into putty and let men take advantage of them.

She shoved her hands into the pockets of her coat. "I think you're right. I need to get back."

"You're sensible, aren't you?" They turned from the lights to walk back to the car.

She thought about the question and how suddenly dumb it was. Yes, she was sensible. And, a moment ago, she'd lost all sensibility. That was what passion and lust did to a person. It was, she now understood, what her mother felt when a man would give her attention. How quickly a gaze or a touch could be misconstrued into something more. Convinced that those things could build into love, it was no wonder women jumped into bed with total strangers. For heaven's sake, her mother had taken it so far as to marry a man within weeks and they'd had her to show for it. Was this what her mother felt each time a man told her she had beautiful eyes? Did she think it was love and worth marrying for? Tabitha sure didn't. As they climbed into the car and drove away, she tried to come up with the right way to tell him they shouldn't see each other again.

# CHAPTER THREE

Tabitha's eyes stung the next morning. Her lack of sleep hadn't helped her looks or her disposition, especially when Brie casually strolled through the door at eight o'clock. She'd abruptly stopped when she walked into the work area and saw Tabitha already elbow deep in chocolate dipped strawberries and petit fours.

"What time did you get here?" she asked as she hung up her coat.

"I've been here since four." The tension in her voice should have had Brie turning and walking out the front door, but, because they'd been friends since childhood, Tabitha knew she'd stay and, after Brie picked at her like a scab, she'd still love her.

"Why so early?" She took her apron from the hook, slid it over her head, and tied it around her waist.

"Because I couldn't sleep. Can you just get those butterflies molded today? I have the chocolate ready so just get busy."

"You are in one snippy mood," Brie offered up as she took the molds from the cupboard and retrieved the clipboard with the order information. "I take it you didn't toss around in the sheets with your date last night?"

Tabitha shot her head up. Her hair fell over her eyes and she blew the stray strands away.

"No matter what I did with my date last night, it's none of your business."

"Wow, you must have been charming. What did he do? Excuse himself from the table and never come back?"

Tabitha took the towel that had been looped around the tie of her apron and was ready to launch it across the room at Brie's head when she heard the chimes over the front door. She huffed out a loud breath as Brie gave her a sly smile over her shoulder as Tabitha walked toward the front of the store.

Brie would be dealt with. Tabitha hated small-minded people as much as she hated Valentine's Day and the impromptu wedding season. But she put on her smile and happily walked to the counter to help the next person, whose purchase would help pay for a vacation. She could still appreciate the value of such a day, monetarily speaking.

Tabitha did all she could to keep the smile as genuine as possible when she saw the round, smiling face of her most profitable customer standing in her store. "Mrs. Banks, what a nice surprise so early this morning."

"Oh, listen to you." The woman actually giggled and tension began to build behind Tabitha's eyes.

Claire Banks shuffled her way to the counter, obviously eye-balling every piece of chocolate in the case. "I'm sure my Preston told you that I've taken on a huge load this

Valentine's Day. He and his two brothers and his sister have all volunteered to help me see to the weddings I have this weekend and next."

"Sure does seem to be a busy season this year." Which Tabitha thought was an understatement considering the number of orders she still had to fill.

"Oh my, it sure does. But I picked up one more," she said with obvious regret. "And they don't want a cake."

"Very untraditional." Tabitha bit the inside of her cheek and tried to remember the smile she was plastering on her face.

"Yes. Well they want Tabitha Chocolates for each guest. One plate per guest, each with four special pieces."

"Mrs. Banks …"

"Oh, I know. I have you already so busy and that's not to mention your mother's wedding or all of your customers. But, I hoped you'd appreciate the business."

Tabitha balled her fists and dug her nails into her palms to keep herself from losing control. How she was going to turn out the orders she already had on the board was beyond her. And she knew herself well enough to know it was about quality and repeat business – and the almighty dollar.

"Of course we can accommodate you. If you'll just fax me over all of the details …"

"Oh, you're the best." Claire Banks reached over the counter and grabbed for Tabitha's hands. "Thank you."

"It's no trouble," she said through gritted teeth.

"Okay." Claire turned to leave. "I'll send over the information. In fact, I won't fax it but will send it with Preston. He said he was going to stop by and see you today. Said you had a wonderful time last night." She smiled widely. "Oh, isn't new love grand? Such a wonderful time of year for it too. Bye."

Tabitha had taken a breath to stop the woman from her delusions, but it had stuck in her throat as the woman went on and on as she walked out the door.

"New love? Well, I didn't see that one coming." Brie said from behind her.

"Shut up. Just shut up!" Tabitha spun on her heels. "I told the man I never wanted to see him again. I said we weren't a good pair. We didn't have anything in common. That all this crap about Valentine's Day and love at first sight was – well, crap. If it didn't make me so much money, I wouldn't even carry special chocolates for it."

"Wow, you must have been a load of fun last night. No wonder you lost a whole night's sleep over it."

There were many reasons not to hire your best friend. Having them toss back everything you said was one of them. Tabitha was seriously considering Brie's termination, but then thought better about it. She'd can her after Mother's Day and the June wedding season.

Tabitha worked diligently all day, keeping her head down and her hands dredged in decadent chocolate. She'd single-handedly molded, formed, and dipped more chocolate than both of them had in a week. It kept her mind occupied and Brie stayed away from her. But each time the door opened, her stomach knotted and her temper flared because she assumed it was Preston Banks walking in.

Brie stayed until they'd locked the doors and cleaned up the workroom. That was why she'd hired her best friend. Without her having to ask, and only having thrown insults her way, Brie knew she needed the help and she'd given it.

They'd been friends long enough that Tabitha knew it was going to cost her a week of vacation for Brie, a dozen roses, a girls' night out, and the eventual confession that she'd enjoyed her date and had wanted Preston Banks to kiss her – and God knows what else.

Tabitha sat at her desk and added up the receipts for the day. It would never cease to amaze her that she could make as much in one day during February as she would the entire month of July.

There was a knock at the door and absentmindedly she stood and walked to the showroom. And, just like the first time she'd laid eyes on him, Preston stood just beyond her door with his hands cupped around his eyes looking in.

The jump in her heart rate made her uncomfortable. What was it that made her want to pull open the door and envelope him in her arms? He was still a stranger, she reminded herself. She didn't believe in things like falling in love at first site.

Tabitha sucked in a breath and let it out. She didn't love him. Where had that come from?

She unlocked the door and pulled it open, making sure her eyes were narrow and her stance strong. "I expected you much earlier." Her tone was furious just as she'd meant it to be.

"I'm so sorry if you've been waiting." His forehead had wrinkled up and the dip of his head let her know his apology was sincere.

Softness, almost on the verge of sadness, filled his voice and it immediately softened her. That was always her problem. As tough and insensitive as she wanted to be, she didn't like to see eyes of worry.

"It was no problem. Come in." Tabitha waited for him to walk through. The cold drifted in with him chilling her as she shut and locked door. "Temperature dropped."

"It's frigid." Preston reached inside of his coat and pulled out a manila envelope. "Here are the orders from my mother."

"Thank you." She took them, their fingers touching. "You're frozen." She took his hand and pulled him toward the back. "I have a fresh pot of coffee. Let me get you a cup."

Preston followed her to her office as he pulled off his coat and draped it over the chair. She looked up at him and thought he looked tired. Trouble seemed to shadow his eyes and the corners of his lips had turned down.

She poured coffee into a new mug. "Do you take anything in it?"

"Black is fine."

She handed him the mug and returned to her seat behind her desk. "I was just closing my books for the day. I'll need to come in extra early tomorrow to start on the chocolates for the weddings this weekend. I don't know how your mother does it." She was annoying herself with the sound of her own voice, but he just stared at her. "What's wrong?"

"I enjoy watching you." His eyes had lightened and the lines in his face were softening. "I waited to come by. I don't know if I was waiting for you not to be here, or if I just wanted time to think about what I was going to say to you."

Tabitha folded her hands under the desk and rested them in her lap. She hadn't been kind the night before when she'd told him under no circumstances did she want to see him again.

Preston set his mug on her desk and sat in the chair opposite her. "I wanted to apologize for my behavior last night. Perhaps I was a bit too forward asking you to dinner and taking you to look at the lights."

Really? He was worried about dinner? "I didn't mean to make you think that. You were a gentleman." She stood from behind her desk. "It's just - well, I'm not very good relationship material."

Preston stood and rose above her, making her shift her eyes up to his. "Perhaps you'll have to fill me in on that."

"On what?"

"What makes you so bad in a relationship?"

Her words were swelling in her throat as he looked at her with his dark eyes from across the desk. No man had ever stumped her into silence. "It would be more of the track record of my mother that leads me away from relationships." She placed her hands on the desk to steady herself, but only found that she was leaning in closer to him. "I just don't see relationships as very useful."

"Useful." He lifted his hand to her cheek. "I've never heard of relationships referred to in that way."

His hand caressed her skin, and her thinking had become foggy. His skin had warmed from the coffee mug, but there was still that bite of chill as he touched her. She watched as he moved in closer to her, over the top of her desk, and her paperwork slid from under her hands.

The corner of his mouth turned up as he drew her closer to him, his hand still caressing her cheek. "I'm a fairly useful guy. I can run errands. I can sell you a nice car. I can help you with all these orders when you need it."

She could feel his breath on her face as she stretched toward him. God, she wished she could think of something to say, but she wanted him to pull her closer.

Preston stopped, their lips just a whisper apart. "I can also turn your heart upside down. And, Tabitha, I think that might be useful to you."

There was nothing she could say when his lips pressed to hers and heat ripped through her body. Her eyelids closed and color swirled behind them. There was a moan, and she was quite positive it had resonated from her throat, but she couldn't be sure.

His hand tunneled through her hair and rested on the back of her neck. He pulled her closer until her thighs pushed against the edge of the desk.

Tabitha's mind wandered from the paperwork she'd fretted over, now crumbling beneath her fingers, and focused on the man who had her body turning helplessly limp.

Her eyes opened when he pulled back slightly.

His eyes were darker and focused in on hers. "I'd say that was very useful to me."

Tabitha swallowed hard and tried to pull back, but his hand was still on the back of her neck and he prevented her escape. "We can't …"

"We can."

"I just met you."

"Nothing wrong with that."

"Your mother …"

"Thankfully isn't here." He trailed a finger down her jaw. "Don't think this over too much."

"I can't help it."

Preston walked around the desk and she fought the urge to back around it.

He reached for her hands and linked his fingers with hers. "I know what you told me last night, and I completely understand your point." He moved in closer to her, brushing his body up next to hers. "But, see, I do believe in romance and love at first sight. I do believe in Valentine's Day and possibilities. I've seen my share of shotgun weddings and happy couples. And, above all else, I don't think it needs to be useful. Just enjoyable."

It almost made sense when he kissed her again. When her arms lifted around his neck, she couldn't conceive any reason not to enjoy the moment. It didn't have to be forever. It only needed to be right now.

His fingers made lazy circles on the small of her back as his lips toyed with hers. "Will you be my date tomorrow?" he asked as he brushed his bottom lip over hers.

"Date?" Her voice was faint.

"I have to run one of the weddings Mom overbooked. And I would love to have the most beautiful woman on my arm when I arrive."

His hands slowly moved up her back and she felt the tension slide out of her shoulders.

Her eyes drifted closed as he kissed her jaw line to her earlobe. "I'll pick you up at three. We have to get there early." He nipped her ear and then took her deep under again with another kiss that cleared her mind.

Preston eased back and rested his forehead to hers. "I have to go." He let out a breath as if regretful that he had to leave. "The wedding colors are purple and gold." He gently kissed her again then walked around the desk and gathered his coat from the chair. "Save a dance for me," he said with a wink as he slid his arms through his coat and then let himself out of the store.

Tabitha stood in her office alone and waited for the fog which clouded her head to let up. The warmth drained from her body and her eyes once again could focus. Then the anger built in her.

He'd done it to her again.

She fell into her chair and let her arms fall to her sides. She'd known the man for a mere three days and, in that time, he'd maneuvered her into two dates and kissed her absolutely senseless. Well, she wasn't going to settle for it. She wasn't going to let him do that to her.

Her lips still tingled. She pressed her fingers to them and let out a sigh.

It wasn't so bad kissing a man and making plans. Was it so horrible to want to spend the evening with him?

Tabitha pushed back her hair and dropped her head onto her arms atop the desk. She wished she had someone other than her lovesick mother and her overly flirtatious best friend with whom to discuss Preston Banks. Even more, she wished she didn't enjoy him at all.

Tabitha was sure not to give too much away when Brie ran through the door nearly an hour late the next morning. Her objective was to keep a cool head about herself, her mind on her work, and her mouth shut as much as possible.

She'd brought a dress and hung it away in the small closet where she'd hung her coat and stored her purse. Knowing she had a makeup bag, stashed in a canvas bag with her flat iron and bottle of hairspray, gave her an uneasy feeling. She didn't usually put that much thought into a date.

"You're lost in space," Brie said as she stood before her with her hands fisted on her hips. "I've been here ten minutes. I'm an hour late. And you've put swirls on twenty chocolates without a word. What's wrong?"

Tabitha shrugged her shoulders. "Why should there be anything wrong?"

Brie studied her. Tabitha did all she could to keep her face rigid and unreadable, but when the corners of Brie's mouth turned up into a smile she knew she'd been pegged.

In one swift move, Brie stood next to her on the same side of her prep table. "He came back after all." Her voice was airy and her eyes had gone soft. That was exactly the look Tabitha was hoping she didn't have on her own face.

"He did. He had the orders from his mother."

Brie took Tabitha's face in her hand and studied her closer. "He kissed you this time. Not just a peck, but not a full blown make-out session either." She narrowed her eyes as she turned Tabitha's face from side to side. "No, but he kissed you until your head was empty."

Tabitha batted away her hand. "What's gotten into you?"

"Me? Nothing. I'm hopeless. However," she said as she sat on the stool, "you've finally got a sparkle in your eye."

Tabitha batted her eyes as if it would fade that very sparkle. But the way her stomach jumped and her heart skipped she knew the sparkle wasn't fading.

She'd thought of the kisses he'd laid on her lips all night long. When she'd wake, she'd find that she'd pressed a pillow to her body and had wrapped her arms around it because she'd been dreaming of Preston Banks. She was certainly in unfamiliar territory.

Pushing back her shoulders, she lifted her head. "We have a back log that should take us till Easter. Why don't you get an order board and start working."

"What kind of friend are you if you won't share your stories with me?" Brie walked to the wall lined with clipboards and orders to fill. "You could do worse, and you have," she reminded her. "Preston Banks is no slouch."

Tabitha swallowed the lump in her throat. No, he was no slouch. He was tall, dark, and handsome with a firm build under those clothes. The few moments when he'd brushed up against her she'd felt the hard lines of him, and she'd dreamed about what he looked like and how he felt.

She shook her head and tried to focus on the thousand caramels she was putting ornate swirls on. It was an uneasy feeling that crept over her when she looked up and Brie was smiling widely now. "He's hooked you. I think for the first time in your life you've been blindsided by a man."

"I've been blindsided by a man before."

"Not like this." Brie walked back toward Tabitha. "You've been hurt. You've always been the one to walk away, and you've been very careful not to let your mother's ideas of love cloud your head." She took a step back. "But when it hits you, honey, there's no turning away. Love at first sight is real."

The lump that had caught in her throat became a lead ball and dropped right into her stomach. She laid down the icing tube and sat on the stool behind her. Dear Lord, she'd gone and tumbled into exactly what she despised.

# CHAPTER FOUR

Because she was doing everything possible to ease her mind and her body, Tabitha, again, had single handedly filled most of the day's orders. One thing about chocolate, though, you couldn't do too much too fast or the quality, taste, and look of the final project was doomed.

Brie had been gracious enough to banter with small talk about her own recent love life mishaps. The blind date had been terrific. The setup from her mother had lasted three hours before she ditched him at the restaurant. And, of course, it wouldn't be Brie if she hadn't fallen madly in love with the clerk at the movie rental place where she'd gone to return the copy of *When Harry Met Sally* for Tabitha.

Brie dusted her hands on her apron. "Sex in public places is awesome. You could hear the guy at the counter getting angrier the longer he had to stand there. But, oh, it was so worth it."

"What was his name?"

"The mad customer?"

Tabitha grunted out a curse. "No, the guy from the movie store."

Brie shrugged. "John. No, Jim. Maybe it was Todd. Guess I'll have to go back and find out. I really like him." She gave her a wink and Tabitha shook her head. She knew she'd been seeing him longer than she led on, but Brie played it well. She'd been with enough men and had enough one-night stands that it wouldn't surprise Tabitha if she couldn't get the man's name right.

One thing was for sure. She didn't understand casual sex. Why risk everything it had to offer? She wasn't against sex if you'd known someone a reasonable amount of time. After all, she wasn't a complete prude. But there had to be an established relationship of some kind. Then there had to be time when you simply felt things out. Once some guidelines were established then you could go and pick out the condoms that would work best. If he wanted to spring for a nice dinner that was a bonus, but the luxurious hotel room was just as good. Then – she cringed – you had the mechanical, preplanned, sexual encounter you expected.

She looked up at Brie who was dancing to some beat on the radio as she moved the small petit four cakes from the tray to the icing rack. There was a glow to her. There was a free movement in her body.

Tabitha looked down at herself and saw rigid lines.

How had they become friends and stayed that way? They were nothing alike. In fact, when she thought of it, Brie and her mother were very much alike. They tumbled in and out of love and didn't seem to be but momentarily phased by it. The only time Tabitha could have said she was in love, she was hurt. It was just one more reason to not believe in all the hype.

But she liked being happy. Wasn't that some of the reason she chose a career that brought such happiness to others? She loved the look of it. The sounds of it. And she was fairly sure she knew what it felt like. There had been plenty of happiness pumping through her body while Preston Banks pressed against her the night before.

Tabitha bit her lip because suddenly she wanted to share the evening with Brie, but it would blow out of proportion. It would become something it wasn't. But she was bursting.

"I'll need to have you stay and finish the last of the orders tonight," she finally blurted out after the better part of an hour had been silent.

"Sure, whatever." Brie boxed up fine chocolates to ship out to other stores.

When Tabitha looked around she realized she had truly created something bigger than she'd ever imagined. The traffic into the store never ceased. Tables were full of candies and chocolate. Orders on clipboards covered the wall and that, too, was added to daily. Had she ever taken the time to look around at it? No, she'd only immersed herself into it – to hide.

Brie finally turned to her waiting for her to finish instructing her on what to do. "Are you feeling okay?"

"Yeah. I was just thinking about how far I've come here. I mean, I used to do chocolates and cakes for fun. Then I was trained and I made a little profit. Then ..."

"Then one of your gracious stepfathers saw potential and you started the legendary Tabitha Chocolates."

"I did." It sounded neatly wrapped into a little package and both of them knew it hadn't been that simple. "How are we going to get all those orders done?"

"My secret weapon will be here when you leave for your date."

"Date?" The sentimental moment was gone. "What are you talking about?"

Brie laughed as she reached for another box to fill. "The dress in the closet. The makeup and hairspray. Claire Banks on the phone half the morning checking on orders and filling me in on what you can't seem to speak about."

"He told his mother?"

"I think, unlike you, he tells his mother everything. If you don't want to think of it as a date, think of it as a business function. Your chocolates. His mother's planning. You'll get to see him in a different element. One he was born into. See how he does under the stress of a bride-to-be. Heaven forbid he has to deal with a mother-in-law or the mother of the bride."

Tabitha let out a little chuckle and then stiffened back up. "I like him."

"I know you do."

"I'm scared to death."

"Enjoy it."

"It's already moved too fast."

"Not fast enough if you ask me." They both turned at her mother's voice from the doorway. "I'd have been married by now." She smiled grandly as if it were something to be proud of.

Any other time Tabitha would have had plenty to say about it. She didn't think her mother should flaunt around claiming to love someone after moments. But after having been in the presence of Preston Banks for only a few mere hours, she was beginning to understand her mother's fascination with finding love. Perhaps her mother would stay in love if she just knew how to harness it.

She took off her coat and hung it up on the hook on the wall next to Brie's. She retrieved an apron and tied it on. "Okay, I'm here to help. Are we making chocolates first, or are we getting her ready for the night of her life?"

"You told her?" Tabitha gasped at Brie.

"It's really no secret, is it? C'mon, we're excited for you."

"Tabby, it's just a date. A working date none the less. It's not your wedding. Or mine," her mother said with a laugh. "You'll survive. Let us enjoy getting you ready."

The air was out of her lungs and her shoulders fell. She might as well let them enjoy themselves because she knew by the end of the night she'd hate herself for agreeing to go at all.

She wouldn't allow them more than forty-five minutes to make her up before Preston arrived. Had she let them, they would have spent the rest of the afternoon primping her and she didn't want it. As it was, she wasn't so sure she wasn't going to be violently ill.

"You're pretty enough to be the bride," her mother offered as she sprayed the last piece of hair into place, and then quickly retracted when Tabitha shot her a look. "You're not the bride. I don't expect you to be the bride. Just enjoy, okay?"

Guilt riddled her body. She couldn't help but be snide in this moment where her mother was so happy. But it was too hard to expect that she'd enjoy it. "I'll try."

"I'm here to help Brie take care of some of those orders. I know Mrs. Banks has you packed and that getting all those boxes packed before Valentine's Day is imperative. I understand this isn't a good time for you to start dating, but, sweetheart, let go a little." Her mother cupped her face in her hands. "I know you've always felt like the adult and you needed to be the one in control, but take it from me. Sometimes it feels good just to let go a little."

She wanted to argue the logic, but the front door to the store opened and she felt that control begin to slip.

Preston stood there in a black suit and purple tie, carrying a bouquet of roses. Every ounce of fight Tabitha might have had drained out of her. His dark eyes took her in and a smile formed on his lips saying he approved of what he saw. "Tabitha, you look amazing."

"Thank you. Brie and Mom did it." It came out more as an accusation.

"No, it's all you. The dress, hair, and makeup are nice, but..."

She felt her knees begin to melt beneath her weight. Practicality needed to replace the absence of thought in her head. As usual, her business was the first thing she thought of. "We have the order all packed up for tonight. It's in the back."

Her mother touched her daughter's arm. "Brie and I will carry it out. I don't want either of you to touch anything. And," she directed her comment to Preston, "when you get to the hotel, you have someone come out and help you carry the boxes into the ballroom."

"Yes, ma'am." When her mother and Brie disappeared into the back, he moved closer to her. "These are for you."

Tabitha took the roses and couldn't help but bury her face in the soft pedals. "Thank you. You didn't have to do that."

"I know. Couldn't help myself."

Tabitha let the scent of his cologne wash over her as she gazed up at him. Lifting herself up onto her toes, she pressed a kiss to his lips and she felt him stagger before his hands came to rest on her hips.

Preston let out a slow, steady breath. "You didn't have to do that."

"Couldn't help myself," she said then bit her lip in a move she knew was as seductive as it felt.

Preston straightened as her mother and Brie walked through the doorway with their arms loaded with white boxes.

"Mind getting that door for us, handsome?" Brie gave him a wink as he did just as he'd been asked and then followed them out to open the trunk of his car.

Very slowly, Tabitha walked into the back room and filled a bucket with water at the sink. She set the roses in it. Then she took deep, deliberate breaths to calm herself. She didn't want to feel the way she felt about Preston, but it didn't seem to matter what she wanted. Just the sight of him had her entire body tensing, and the sparks he ignited in her just couldn't be ignored.

*Let it go, Tabitha. Enjoy the rush.* She tried to reason with herself.

Preston's hands on her shoulders surprised her. She'd been so deep in thought she hadn't heard him walk back through the store.

He brushed a hand over her hair. "Are you ready?"

"Yes, as a matter of fact, I think I am."

As always, the Green Room at the Colorado School of Mines was the perfect venue for a wedding. It was one of Tabitha's favorite places.

"You're smiling." Preston stood beside her as she looked down the grand staircase that let into the large room below her.

"I love this place." There was a peace that filled her when she looked over the dance floor.

He slid his arm around her waist. "What is it that makes it such a happy place?"

Tabitha let out a laugh. "My mother got married here when I was five. She bought me a dress to match hers, and I even got to wear a veil." She let out a sigh as they started their walk down the stairs. "We walked down these stairs together and my stepfather waited at the bottom with the minister. I gave her away."

He reached for her hand and took it in his as they started down the steps. "That's a beautiful memory."

"She had a cake with stairs that led to smaller cakes. It was a theme, I guess. But I always thought if I ever got married, I'd get married here. And I'd have stairs on my cake, too."

Tabitha stepped off the bottom step and looked around the room, which buzzed with people setting up tables and chairs for another couple's wedding.

Preston reached for her arm and spun her to him. "Maybe you'll get your chance to get married here someday."

"No." She shook her head and pursed her lips.

"No? That was a quick answer."

"Weddings are just parties where the guests speculate how long the marriage will last."

"Forty years."

"What?" She looked up at him and he was smiling a broad, white smile.

"My parents have been married for forty years. I can't imagine that people were placing bets on how long it would last."

"Maybe that's only at my mother's weddings then." She took a step back, but he pulled her to him again.

"It doesn't have to be that way for you."

Tabitha looked away from him because she couldn't begin to think of fancy cakes and staircases. She couldn't let herself think in terms of someday. She brought happiness to the weddings she catered with her chocolates. Never would she expect happiness from a wedding to be hers.

When she saw the caterers carrying the boxes of chocolates in, she broke from Preston's grasp and followed them to the table where the cake had been set up. She hadn't been asked to help set up, but she thought it was best to calm her nerves.

She was completely aware that the moment she'd left Preston's side he'd been swept up by a man she assumed was the father of the bride. She didn't see him again until the wedding ceremony was over and the reception had begun.

He moved in next to her as she stood against the wall and watched as the bride and groom took their first dance.

"Sorry, I'm not a very good date," he apologized, lifting her hand to his lips and pressing a kiss into her palm.

"I've been watching you work. You're a people person and you have a good eye for detail."

"From someone who works with details, I'll take that as a compliment. However, I think the bride would have preferred my mother when she broke down right before the ceremony."

Tabitha turned to him. "She did?"

"It's not uncommon. They get wrapped up in the details, and the emotion of what the wedding means gets lost. It just takes a little coaching to work them through it."

"And you did that for her?"

He straightened the knot of his tie. "It's all part of my service."

She could imagine, as he was called off to handle yet another detail, she'd be one of those brides who fretted over the wrong things. Would someone like Claire Banks come to rescue her and put her mind at ease? Would it all be okay after softly spoken words?

Preston ducked into the hallway with the caterer, and Tabitha shook her head. It was silly thoughts like that which had women swooning in February.

She shook it off, found a vacant seat at a table in the corner, and watched the merriment that surrounded her.

The bride and groom had left in a grand farewell, and the guests that lingered were few. Caterers began to pack up their items, and the crews started to take down the tables and chairs. Preston crossed the room, his suit jacket draped over his arm.

"Hey, lady, did your date leave you?"

She looked around the room. "It would appear he did."

He laid his jacket over the back of a chair and reached his hand for hers pulling her to her feet. "Unacceptable. I'll bet he didn't even dance with you."

"Nope, and the DJ seems to have packed up."

He pulled her arm spinning her against him and wrapped his other hand around her waist. "I hear music, Tabitha."

"You do?" She moved with him in the silent dance.

"Every time I see you, I hear music."

Romantic words. That's where it always started.

He pulled her closer until her face pressed against his chest. She settled close to him. It wasn't so bad.

She felt his lips in her hair as his hand caressed her back. "I realize its past midnight, but I would love to take you out for breakfast when we're done here."

"Breakfast? I don't think I can refuse. I'm starving."

He let out a laugh. "Good, so am I."

She lifted her arms around his neck as he moved in slow, rhythmic circles. She pulled her head back to look up at him. "Tomorrow is going to be a long day."

"Do you have to work?"

"One week until Valentine's day. Yes, I have to work."

"I'll help you."

"Is there anything you don't do? Sell cars, calm brides, make chocolates." She swung her hair so that it brushed her back.

"I have many talents." He tilted her chin with his finger. "Someday I'd like to show you some of my other talents."

Tabitha swallowed hard. How could she not read trouble into that?

# CHAPTER FIVE

Tabitha was still exhausted from Saturday night. With a clearer mind, she decided she was more tired from Sunday morning. Their night hadn't ended until almost noon when he'd brought her back to the store. He'd stayed until he watched her drive away, making her keep her promise to not go into the store nor touch a thing. They'd made a deal, neither of them would work. They were both to head home and straight to bed.

She hadn't talked to him since they'd parted with a satisfying kiss, but it was well into her thirty-fifth hour of being awake before she could calm her head and rest. He filled her mind and she couldn't shake it, no matter how hard she tried, so she didn't. Finally, she fell asleep dreaming of him.

She took great pride in herself for still getting to work before the sun and, for the first time in years, she worked with a smile on her face that didn't come from her successes as a chocolatier but from being a woman happy because of a man.

The workroom of the store buzzed with work. Her mother had come to help, Brie was there with her music playing, and her mother's fiancée had gone on the coffee run. He'd volunteered to work the front counter, swearing it would be better for them all if that was all the help he offered.

Tabitha toyed with the idea of bringing in a few more hands for the last week before Valentine's Day. With a glance at the order boards, she just wasn't sure how she'd manage it all with just Brie, especially if Brie decided this was a good week to fall in love, again.

She continued to roll balls that would become decadent truffles when the front door opened.

"Tabitha, are you back there?" She heard Claire Banks' voice carry through the store, and then there she was standing in the doorway. "Well, look at all this work going on. I'm glad I came by."

"Good morning, Mrs. Banks. How are you?"

"I'm wonderful. How are you? Preston says you danced past midnight and had a lovely breakfast."

Tabitha smiled at the memory of dancing in the silent hall she adored. "Yes, we did."

"I've already received calls," she said turning toward the pegs on the wall and hanging up her coat. "The couple had the very best day of their lives and the father of the bride said it was a magical night. Preston did a fine job of keeping things running smoothly. Word is he even calmed an anxious bride."

"He mentioned it."

"If I could just convince him to work with me and stop selling cars, I'd have one heck of a partner." Claire took a white apron from a hook and tied it around her wide body. "You helped me. I'm here to help you. Put me to work."

Tabitha stopped rolling the truffle and set it down on the tray. She couldn't help but just stare at Claire Banks standing before her in an apron that hardly covered her. She hadn't asked for help. In fact, her own mother wouldn't be there had Brie not called her.

"Mrs. Banks, really you don't need to ..."

"Darling, this is what people do. If someone is sick, you take them dinner. When a mother looks like she's about to drop from exhaustion, you take her kids for the afternoon. When your favorite chocolatier has chocolates for weddings you begged her to take on, a major holiday coming up, her own mother's wedding, and dinner with a very handsome man, you step up."

The workload she'd mentioned was enough to shake her. However, it was the end of that sentence that had her muscles tightening. "I have dinner plans?"

"You will." Claire was absolutely beaming. Her smile was so wide it made the apples of her cheeks pink with color. "He'll be along shortly."

Multiple emotions struck out at Tabitha. There was too much to do to think about men coming to take her to dinner unexpectedly. She had orders to finish. Molds to fill. Heart shaped boxes to ship.

But then there was the conflict. Wouldn't it be nice to blow off the day and spend it wrapped in the arms of a handsome man kissing him senseless?

God, this wasn't like her. She couldn't focus on one thought and she'd always been able to do that. And that thought had always been work.

When Preston walked through the door, she knew which one she wanted more and she'd never been one to lax on her business owner responsibilities. And when he shot her a look that told her his mind had wandered to the same place hers had, it felt as though they were the only two in the room.

Preston broke eye contact when his mother crossed to him. "I told her you'd be here soon." Claire kissed him on the cheek.

"I didn't know you'd be here."

"As I told her, she helped me and I'm here to help her."

Preston lifted his eyes back to her. "Well, then, where do I get one of those fancy aprons?"

What the heck, Tabitha decided. At least the view would be nice while she finished her work.

Since eyes were on her from the moment Preston walked through the door, Tabitha decided she might as well work side by side with him. Let them have their foolish giggles and whispers. For the moment, she was just going to enjoy how he made her feel because she knew it was never going to last.

He was an attentive student.

There wasn't any task she'd given him that was too complicated. But, as she'd told him at the wedding, he had an eye for detail. Before her were dozens of truffles which she hadn't rolled. Her fingers would surely thank her later when they didn't cramp up by just holding the fork during dinner.

The morning moved into afternoon. They rolled truffles, decorated petit fours, dipped caramels, and piped tiny flowers onto all of them. She'd assigned jobs by their abilities and did her best to let go of the need to have everything as perfect as she'd have made it.

Her mother and her mother's fiancée left after lunch to attend to wedding details. Brie had a date with the clerk from the movie rental store. She'd been good on her word to find out his name and remember it. It was John. When Preston's father called looking for his wife, Claire said goodbye, kissed them both, and left smiling as widely as she had been when she'd walked in.

Preston let out a large sigh. "I thought they'd never leave."

Tabitha tucked in her smile and felt the heat rush through her. "I've never had that much help before. I think we are actually on schedule."

"Good. Then you can enjoy your evening."

The smile Tabitha had wanted to hide diminished. Enjoy her evening? He didn't use the phrase, "we can enjoy our evening." Hadn't Claire mentioned that she'd be having dinner with him?

She turned to set the tray of chocolates on the drying rack. The beautiful hearts she'd just piped on to each of them were suddenly as ugly as the mood that brewed inside of her. This was why attraction was so hard. It led to feelings that weren't real. Why should she care if he had other plans? What did it matter if she'd misunderstood his mother? She had plenty to do. Sure, they were on schedule, but she could be far ahead of schedule.

The racks of trays clanked together as she pushed them into the room she kept cool enough so that the chocolate would dry, but not cloud in the cold of a refrigerator.

She closed the door to the small room and turned to stare in disbelief at the man who waited for her with his jacket already on and hers held in his hands.

She cleared her throat. "Are you leaving?"

"I didn't ask, but I was hoping you'd join me."

She looked him over as she walked toward him. She hadn't noticed how he'd been dressed when he'd walked through her door. He wasn't dressed as though he'd come from work. A faded pair of Levi's and a simple black, button down shirt was not usual work attire for a luxury car salesperson. He'd taken his day off, or had taken the day off, and shown up to help her make candies. She'd never thought to ask why he wasn't working on a Monday. The warmth of the gesture melted her anger.

He'd already put on his worn leather jacket, and Tabitha hated that she wanted to run to him and wrap her arms around him. How much sexier could the man get?

He shook her coat in his hands. "You look lost in thought. I'm not thinking anything fancy, but I have a hankering for some pizza."

"Pizza sounds great. Give me a minute to freshen up?"

He draped her coat over his arm. "Sure."

Consciously, she tried to only take a few moments in the bathroom putting herself together, but she was lost in the image in the mirror. Looking back at her should have been the face of the same woman she'd been staring at for thirty years. The face had matured, sure, but it had never quite had the glow to it she saw now.

Tabitha touched her cheeks. Was it just her or did the world see that glow? She swallowed hard.

She was successful. She was still young. But that wasn't it.

Only a moment later, she watched as her own brown eyes grew wide at her reflection. She'd seen that glow before, only never on her own face. No, she'd seen it on her mother's face. She'd seen that sparkle in Brie's eyes.

It was love.

Panicked, she turned on the cold water and ran her hands under it. Then she scrubbed her face and looked back into the mirror. But even with her skin dripping, the glow was there.

She'd gone and fallen in love, which was exactly what she hadn't wanted to do.

The pizza parlor was as far from fancy as he could have gotten. The plastic, red gingham tablecloths and metal chairs with red vinyl seats comforted her. It reminded her of many of the places her mother had taken her when she was young. They never would have frequented the sushi restaurant Preston had taken her to before.

Preston had seated them in the corner booth, just under the television that hung from the ceiling. A hockey game played, but she'd never really understood the game well enough to know what was going on.

He handed her a copy of the menu that was posted on a board above the counter. "I have to order at the counter. Is there anything you don't like on your pizza?"

"Not really." She looked over the toppings list. "Oh, wait. You're not one of those men who have to have fish or anything like that on their pizza, are you?"

"I love sausage, mushroom, and green peppers on my pizza. But I can eat anything you want."

"Actually I think that sounds nice." She tucked the menu back behind the shakers of crushed red peppers and cheese.

"Coke or beer?"

"What are ..."

He chuckled, cutting off her sentence. "I'm having a beer. Why don't I just get us a pitcher."

"For just the two of us?"

"Lightweight," he joked as he walked to the counter to order.

Tabitha looked around the quaint restaurant. There were only a few tables, and small children occupied one of them. The owner's kids, she assumed. One read, another colored, and the boy played a video game with headphones covering his ears to block out the world.

A man yelled through a window the order he needed and then would toss the pizza just behind the counter. A family run restaurant, what a pleasure that was.

Why had she never been there? It was only two miles from her shop and within a ten-mile radius of all the houses she'd grown up in.

She set her elbows on the table and rested her chin in the palms of her hands. Had she gone and isolated herself so much that, when she gave it some thought, she didn't know the area around her very well at all?

Preston returned with two glasses and the pitcher of beer. He set it on the table and took a seat next to her in the high backed booth. He looked up at the television and winced.

"Damn. Did you see that puck hit that guy in the chest? Do you know what kind of mark that makes? You have to really love playing a game to risk injury." He poured her beer and then poured one for him. "This place has the best calzones." He took a sip from his glass. "We used to frequent this joint in college."

"Where'd you go?"

"University of Denver. How about you?"

Tabitha shook her head. "I didn't have the opportunity. Stepdad number three took off with all of mom's savings. Needless to say that meant my college education."

"Sorry." He placed his hand over hers and gave it a squeeze. "No wonder you're not a big fan of her getting married."

"They weren't all bad. And Peter seems to be a nice guy." She shrugged. "You just can't help but wonder for how long."

"You don't think this is the one?"

Tabitha laughed. "God, no. Is there really just such a thing for anyone?"

His hand stiffened over hers and then he pulled it away. "My parents have been married forty years. They fell in love at fifteen."

"I think that's very special, but not the norm."

"My father's parents were married for fifty years before my grandfather died. My mother's parents have been married almost seventy years."

She gave it some consideration, but she couldn't think of anyone in her family who'd stayed married. Her grandmother was a single mother. She didn't know her father's parents. Even Brie's parents were divorced and remarried. Obviously the marriages Preston spoke of were flukes of luck.

Preston sat back against the booth and looked her over as he drank his beer. "How come you went into a business that feasts on people's happiness?"

His tone offended her and she stiffened her shoulders. "I like what I do."

"I know that. I mean, you buy a Snickers bar if you're depressed. Or you buy a pint of Ben and Jerry's. You don't go to Tabitha Chocolates and buy expensive truffles to drown your sorrows. You buy Tabitha Chocolates for people you love. You buy them to impress people or to show them you care."

"I'm good at what I do. That's why I do it."

"You are. But you're so hell bent on love and relationships being such a bad thing, doesn't it depress you every day to see people happy."

Tabitha puckered her lips and shook her head. "Just because I don't believe in love and marriage doesn't mean I'm not a happy person."

"But how can you sell your creations, which you put your heart into, to people celebrating something you don't believe in?"

"It's what I do." Who was he to question her motives for her work? She didn't ask him why he chose luxury cars over used ones on some street corner, though she knew he'd fallen into the field, but the point was he'd stayed and made it his life's work.

"Tell me, Tabitha," he said as he lifted his hand to her cheek. "What makes you happy?"

Her mind drew a blank as she stared into his dark eyes. That very moment should have made her happy, shouldn't it have? Why did she feel she had to fight him off?

The waitress arrived with the pizza and Preston backed away from her and smiled up at the woman. "That looks wonderful."

She dished them each out a slice onto a paper plate and headed back to the kitchen.

Preston carefully picked up the hot slice, which strung cheese from the plate to his mouth. "Oh, you're going to love this," he said trying to bite into the hot pizza.

Tabitha looked at the large slice of pizza on her plate. Her appetite seemed to have diminished.

She couldn't help but notice everything that surrounded her was about love, and she hadn't completely realized it before. The very word made her nervous. How many times had he said the word love since they'd walked into the restaurant? He loved the pizza and the restaurant itself. Hockey players loved playing hockey, his grandparents were in love, his parents were in love – he never quit.

What was she missing?

Love was everywhere. If it weren't for that stupid four-letter word, even her business wouldn't exist.

Preston nudged her with his elbow. "Are you all right? Your face is pale."

"Fine. I'm fine." She chugged at her beer until she felt it numb her face. She couldn't hide from it. Love was everywhere and it had invaded her heart.

Tabitha lifted her eyes to Preston's. What would happen if she fell in love with him and was honest about it? She set down her glass and lifted her hands to cup his face.

He was the most handsome man she'd ever met and very sincere. What if she were to be carefree for once in her life? Would it kill her? Would it end as quickly as it started?

His eyes were gentle, his mouth welcoming, and his hands sent surges of electricity through her veins every time he touched her. What would it be like to let this man into her life to smile at her every day and say beautiful things? She wanted it. She was buying into it. It might just kill her, but she wanted it.

Tabitha pulled him to her and took possession of his mouth. The beer swam in her head as she sank into the kiss.

His hands moved slowly up her arms and warmth pulsed through her. It wasn't the time or place, but she wanted more. Instead, she eased back and he was smiling at her.

"You are full of surprises," he said. His hands lingered on her arms.

"You make me feel things I don't want to feel." There, she'd admitted it.

He didn't look away. "Give it a try, Tabitha. Romance. Love. Forever. It's not so scary if you just believe."

"I can only offer you the moment."

"That's all I want." He lifted his hand to her hair and brushed it away from her face. "The moment I saw you standing behind the counter of your store I felt something I'd never felt before. I would have come in everyday if it meant seeing you. I got lucky. You let me take you to dinner."

"I didn't want to go. I wasn't going to be there when you came for me."

"I know. Sometimes fate steps in." She tried to lean away from him, but he kept his hands on her. "Don't let it frighten you. No matter what, I won't hurt you."

She was sure of it. But she was damn sure she was going to hurt him.

# CHAPTER SIX

On Tuesday, Tabitha didn't have time to think of sexy men and quaint, pizza dinners. She didn't have time to dwell on the slight headache from the beer she'd drank or the kisses she'd pressed to Preston's lips. Not on her mind at all were the kisses they'd shared when he drove her home and forced himself to leave after they'd made out like a couple of kids on the couch. And there was a gratefulness that after she'd asked Brie to pick her up to take her to work, Brie had asked for the day off without many questions as to why her car was still at the shop.

Yes, she was glad to be busy and not be thinking of anything. And luckily, Preston was busy selling cars today too and didn't have time for her either. However, his mother decided that her store was a good place to spend her days now that her son seemed smitten with Tabitha.

"This is more fun than I ever could have imagined," Claire said as she dipped a strawberry. "What patience you have."

"I enjoy what I do."

"So do I. I love to see the faces of the couples when they come in and tell me what they are looking for." Claire skillfully dipped another strawberry. "I can tell when a couple isn't going to make it. But, for the most part, they are all so in love when they come to see me and it just makes my heart so happy."

Tabitha watched as Claire continued to dip strawberries as though it had been her calling in life. At least if wedding planning stopped being so successful, Tabitha knew she could hire her to help out. She was trained to have an eye for detail.

Watching her, however, wasn't taking her mind off of what Claire had said. She enjoyed other people's happiness and it made her happy. That Tabitha understood. She'd seen her mother's face the first time she'd baked her a cake in that little light bulb oven. It was a pleasure she'd never seen on anyone else's face.

But it was different now. People who bought her chocolates bought them so they could see that pleasure on their loved ones faces, but she wasn't accustomed to seeing it at all anymore. Oh, there were smiles and shrills of delight, but not that same kind of emotion brought on because of someone else.

She thought of the wedding she'd attended with Preston. The bride and groom had that kind of pleasure on their faces. The kind that told her that the wedding itself wasn't important. It was a formality. What was important was they would be together forever.

With a little more thought, she realized she'd seen that look on Preston's face as he'd danced her around the floor in her bare feet.

The clanging of the spoon she'd had in her hand hitting the metal table was enough to snap her back to reality.

Claire was still talking, but Tabitha hadn't heard a word she'd said. She picked up the spoon and continued to stir together the sugar mixture she'd sprinkle over the strawberries.

"Don't you love that, too?" Claire asked her and she snapped her head up.

"Love what?"

"How happiness is contagious, and you just want to be part of it?"

Tabitha put down the spoon and wiped her sweaty palms along her apron. Yes, she did want to be a part of it, but she'd fought it for so long she didn't know how to be happy anymore. Even Claire Banks sitting a mere three feet from her, grinning from ear to ear just talking about it, made Tabitha break out into a sweat. She'd forgotten how to be happy. Or maybe she'd never been happy.

Well, it was obviously too late for her now. She couldn't even make herself be happy on cue. That was it. Preston didn't deserve her. It was off for good - even if it had never really started. She picked the spoon back up and began to assault the sugar. All the better, he'd better know now that she was a miserable person and move on. It wasn't going to change anytime soon.

Tabitha closed shop on time, leaving orders undone that she should have filled, and headed straight home. The moment she walked through the door, she kicked her shoes off and left a trail of clothes all the way down the hall and into the bathroom where she turned on the shower to hot. Not only was it freezing outside, she was freezing on the inside. Self-doubt and pity would do that to a person. She was angry that she'd let herself even get so deep into her emotions.

Deliberately, she chose the mint shampoo and conditioner and washed away the flour in her hair and the tension from her scalp. She picked the lavender body wash to calm her tense, tight skin brought on by worry. The scent of cocoa washed away and her body eased back in to normal Tabitha mode.

The sad, pathetic shell of someone who didn't want to feel anything.

Still dripping wet and naked, she stepped up to the mirror. She wiped away the steam that clouded her view. A tear broke free and streaked down her cheek as she gazed at the reflection. Why had he even given her a second glance?

Though the person in the mirror was her, she didn't like what she saw. Sunken eyes, pale skin, and a frown tugged the edges of her mouth down. It was the same reflection she'd seen for years. But she'd never noticed how pathetic it was.

If Preston was even one-tenth of the wonderful person his mother was, he didn't deserve someone like her.

Tabitha reached for her robe and tied it around her body. She grabbed a comb and yanked it through her hair. Preston always wore a smile and, even though he talked fast, he never had anything bad to say. She looked in the mirror again. When he gazed into her eyes, was this what he saw?

A warm pair of flannel pajamas and warm fuzzy socks did little to warm her. She brewed a cup of tea and plopped herself down on the couch. Maybe some sappy movie would make the evening tolerable.

She began flipping through channels until she came upon *You've Got Mail.* One of her favorites. No one could cheer her up better than Tom Hanks.

The tune to the opening credits already had her easing back in her seat. She lifted the tea to her lips just as there was a knock at the door. She jumped and hot tea spilled down the front of her. She flew to her feet and strung a slew of curses together as she fanned the wet flannel from her burning skin.

"Hold on. Hold on!" She yelled at the person continuing to pound at the door.

Tabitha set the tea on the coffee table and ran to the kitchen for a towel to stop the burning she felt against her flesh. As soon as the sting muted a bit, she headed for the door to sock the person in the jaw who had the nerve to summons her from the couch and make her burn herself.

She swung the door open to the wall of cold outside. As the door opened, the person leaning on it fell inside.

Tabitha jumped back. "What are you doing?"

"Sorry." Preston stumbled to gain his balance on his feet. "I was so tired I was leaning on the door. I didn't expect it to swing open like that."

"Why did you just keep knocking?"

"It's what you do to get someone to open the door, especially when it's ten below outside. Now can we close it?" He grabbed hold of the door and shut it against the cold, bitter wind that pushed against it.

His face was red from the wind that had battered pellets of ice against his skin. The whites of his eyes were red, and dark circles told her he hadn't slept well.

The wet towel in her hand, the pajamas which smelled like tea, and the burn now stinging again on her chest reminded her that she didn't care if he'd slept, she was still mad. She hadn't invited him over and he shouldn't be there.

She turned and walked back to the kitchen to retrieve a dry towel. "What do you want?"

"What do I want? I wanted to see you." Preston followed her and, when she stood from reaching in the drawer for a towel, he was right there behind her. She slammed her face into his chest and knocked them both back.

"Why are you right there, too? Geese, get out of my way." She pushed past him.

"You're in a mood. Don't I even get a hello kiss?"

Tabitha spun around. "A hello kiss? Who do you think you are?"

"I thought I was the man who'd missed you all day and wanted to come all the way over here for a kiss. I'm beginning to think I was wrong."

"Way wrong." She pushed the towel to her chest where the burn reminded her how mad she was at him.

"What's with the towel?"

"I spilled my tea on myself while you beat down my door."

He moved swiftly to her. "I'm so sorry. Are you hurt?"

Tabitha took a step back only to find herself pinned in with her back against the refrigerator door. "It's just a ... well, a little burn." Her breath hitched as he lifted a hand to the collar of her pajamas.

"Let me see."

She couldn't use words. She shook her head. No, she had to move away from him. But her feet were planted.

"Tabitha, I want to check. Do I need to take you to a doctor?"

"No," she said, but it was much too airy. Her head fell back against the refrigerator as Preston unbuttoned the top of her pajamas and parted the fabric.

He trailed his finger down her skin, stopping where redness marked her just between her breasts. Tabitha closed her eyes and her breath caught. When she opened them, he was staring at her. That twinkle was in his eyes and the corner of his mouth lifted.

"Something tells me you're not hurting too bad."

Tabitha narrowed her stare at him. "I'm fine." She tried to step forward, but he was too close.

"Let me make it all better." He lowered his lips to her neck and she felt her knees turn soft. He pressed kisses to her collarbone and Tabitha pushed her palms against the cold, metal door behind her to keep from sliding to the floor.

Preston trailed kisses to the burn just at the junction where the swells of her breast parted. Her eyes fell closed, and she sucked in a breath when he unfastened the next button on her pajamas.

"Preston, I'm fine." Her voice was just a whisper, a weak protest for him to stop. But he didn't.

The next button had been released and the flannel parted. Preston cupped her breasts in his hands and kissed each one of them, sucking her nipple between his lips. Heat shot through her from her groin up through her to her chest. The breath she had taken in whooshed from her lungs as her hands came off the door and to his head. She tangled her fingers in his hair as he pushed her top from her shoulders. She dropped her arms for a moment and let the shirt fall to the floor before reaching back to him and tangling her fingers in his hair.

Preston's lips were back at hers and she was hungry for him. The protest was over as he nipped her lip, biting down hard enough to send the signal of pain, but when mixed with the pleasure it only stirred the heat inside of her making her hotter. He pulled her legs up around his waist. Tabitha's arms encircled his neck as he carried her to the hall.

Their tongues danced fast and quick, his hands gripped her bottom, and she pulled him to her tighter. He leaned her against the wall and the cold shot through her, forcing her to tear away from him.

"Your room." His mouth was back at hers. "Where's your room?"

She pointed down the hall and he stumbled, with her wrapped around him, to the open door.

The room was dark and she was much too busy to guide him. But when she heard the smack of his leg on the end of the bed and she fell back, she couldn't help but laugh. "Are you alright?"

"I'm fine," he said as he bent over to rub his calf. "Sorry I dropped you."

"I think you meant to."

"Maybe." He walked around the bed and pulled her legs to shift her right in front of him. Her breath caught. For an instant as he looked down at her while unbuttoning his shirt, she wondered what she was doing. This was just how it moved too far too fast. But as his shirt fell away and the hard lines of his chest were shadowed by the light from the hallway, he leaned over her, bracing his hands on either side of her, and their skin touched, and she didn't care how fast it all was moving.

To hell with what she thought about relationships that were carelessly forged, she decided as his chest brushed against her sensitive nipples. Forget that she didn't believe in love at first sight or true love at all, she thought as his mouth moved across her chest. At that moment, all she wanted was Preston Banks to kiss her until she no longer could remember why she didn't believe in love, romance, and happily ever after.

Preston's lips were warm on her skin and his weight pressed down on her. He kissed his way down her neck, between her breasts, and over her stomach as he inched her flannel bottoms off.

He stood just looking down at her. She was naked and exposed to him. "God, you're beautiful." His voice was soft.

Tabitha fought the urge to cover her body which, like his, was lit only by the light from the hallway. She could see in his eyes he wasn't judging her, he wasn't expecting too much of her either, he was strictly admiring her.

What kind of foreplay was this? Her heart squeezed in her chest, and she was afraid it was the worst kind. It was the kind that took you under and you couldn't breathe. The kind that made you worry about someone else for the rest of your life and made you never want to spend a moment apart from him.

She knew what was happening, and even so, she watched as he undressed. Her fingers dug into the comforter as she fought the urge to rip the rest of his clothing from him. As each layer was stripped away, she simply admired the beauty of his skin, his muscles, and his confidence.

He stopped what had been a beautiful strip tease and took a moment to pull his wallet from his pant pocket. He laid it on the bed next to her and then he pressed his naked body to hers.

When she felt his heart beat next to hers, she tumbled farther into that abyss that she'd fought for so long.

Their mouths met again in a fiery kiss that had them each fighting for breath. Their skin, pressed together, heated. Her hands moved down his back and over the curve of his tight bottom. She gave it a squeeze which pushed his erection between her legs and she gasped. She couldn't wait for him any longer. In fact, it wasn't the sex he promised with his hard body pressed to hers. She simply couldn't live without him one moment more.

Preston reached for his wallet and took a condom out from the back.

"You were prepared, huh?" She fought to not make the moment less than it was, but she couldn't help herself.

"Boy scout," he said ripping the wrapper. "But yes. Since the minute I met you, I've been hopefully prepared."

"Oh." Disappointment filled her voice and her stomach clenched. "Is this what you want from me?"

He stopped and his eyes opened wide. "No. No. I'll stop." He shifted. "I mean, don't get me wrong. I want to make love to you more than anything." He looked down between his legs and back up at her. "Obviously. But, Tabitha, what I feel for you is so much more than sex."

"Really?"

He leaned in closer to her. "I know you don't believe in love at first sight, but I do. The moment I looked into those chocolate brown eyes, I was gone."

"You're saying you fell in love with me?"

"I'm saying that's how strong my feelings are for you. Yes." He brushed a stand of hair from her eyes. "I fell in love with you."

God, that was just what she'd expected from him. Now here she was falling into the same trap her mother and Brie fell into too often. A man spoke to her softly and undressed her with gentle hands. He'd covered her body in perfectly placed kisses and now he said he'd fallen in love with her.

But looking at him, she couldn't help but believe him. She wanted to believe that love could come so quickly and last forever. Then again, as he slid his hand over her stomach and it twitched inside, she didn't care. She rolled over and straddled him.

"You love me?" She looked down at him and he gripped her hips.

"Yes."

"And you expect me to fall in love with you?"

"No, but it would be nice."

Tabitha swallowed hard. "I've never been in love before."

"Then I'll take my time with you."

If only she could say the words this would be when they should be said. She wanted to love him. She wanted everything from him.

"Tabitha, we either need to decide to do this or get dressed. You're killing me."

"I want to. I really want to."

"Good." He rolled her over, back onto her back. He took the condom and rolled it on. "I thought I was going to have to go throw myself into a snow bank."

He moved himself on top of her and she reached her hands around to pull him closer. "You make me very happy."

"I'll take that."

"I'm going to screw this up." She bit down on her lip as she felt him ease in closer.

"We both are. That's what love and a relationship is all about."

He pushed inside of her and her head fell back. His arms held her tight and his lips pressed warmly to her throat. She'd done it. She'd fallen in love and she didn't know what to do about it. But as he moved in and out of her, she wrapped her legs around him and urged him deeper. Not just deeper into her body but into her soul. This was what it was about. This was the falling.

As the rhythm picked up and her fingers dug into his flesh, she fought the urge to wonder about the crash. She desperately wanted to enjoy the fall.

Preston pushed her hair back from her face and gazed down at her as she felt every muscle in her body tighten. She bit down on her quivering lip and her breath quickened as his pace grew faster.

"I love you, Tabitha. I want to make you happy."

His eyes drew closed and he dropped his head into the crevice of her neck. The moan that came out might have belonged to her, it might not have. All she knew was she'd never felt like this before. Her body rode a wave of pleasure and, as his body quivered atop of hers, she felt him grip tighter to her as if she were falling away. But in actuality she was falling with him.

Then he lay still and she fought for her breath.

"That was awesome." He whispered on a ragged breath in her ear as he adjusted his weight.

"Was it?"

"Oh, don't shoot me down. Yes, it was." He caressed her face and kissed her. "You didn't think it was awesome?"

"It was." She wanted to cover up feeling the chill of the room and the unmistakable cold of regret. "So many things were running through my head."

Preston rolled off her and lay on his back. "I thought I was better at this. But she's making grocery lists." He beat a little rhythm with his fingers on his chest.

"No." She sat up and the nakedness didn't matter. "No, it wasn't like that. I was accounting for the fact that I'd never fallen in love before. I didn't know what to think. I had to place the feelings. I had to..."

"Wait." The grin on his face was wide, and he sat up to look her in the eyes. "Did you just say what I think you did?"

"I... what?" Oh, he was taking her words and twisting them, but she wasn't really sure what she'd said.

"You said you'd never fallen in love before and you didn't know what to do with the feelings."

"Right, that's what I said. I wasn't making..."

"Shhh." He pressed his lips to hers. "You just said you fell in love with me."

Tabitha took a breath to counter, but realized that was exactly what she'd said. God, she'd just told him, in her own screwed up way, that she loved him.

The room was silent except for the pounding of her own heart resonating through her body. She wasn't cold any longer, now heat engulfed her.

What was she to do? What should she say now?

There wasn't a moment to think about it. He pulled her to her feet and wrapped his arms tightly around her.

"This is different for me, too. I've told women I love them, I won't lie. But I've never felt it like this before." He tangled his hands in her hair and kissed her hard enough that she could feel her teeth cutting into the back of her lips. "This is great."

"Wait." She pressed her palms to his chest to give herself some space, but Preston Banks was a bigger man than she'd even first thought. He wasn't budging anywhere. "But we've only known each other a week."

"Long enough."

"This isn't right." Her tone was defensive and his grin infuriated her.

"Oh, yes it is." He scooped her legs up and carried her around the room, making little circles as he waltzed her to the other side of the bed. "I'm going to make love to you all night, and you're going to have to tell me again and again how much you love me."

Tabitha wrapped her arms around his neck. "Don't push it, Banks."

He laughed and laid her on the bed, looking down at her with a grin that teetered between sexy and funny. "I'll have to take tomorrow off." He took his watch off and laid it on the nightstand.

"Why?"

"Because," he knelt down next to her, "I'm going to make love to you all night until I can convince you to marry me. You'll be too tired to do all that work alone tomorrow."

"Convince me of what?" She sat up and smacked heads with him. She cursed. He laughed.

"C'mon, Tabitha. Fall a little further." He lowered her back to the bed. "You don't have to rationalize this." He traced her lips with his finger and then with his tongue. "Fall, Tabitha. Fall in love with me." He rolled on top of her and began making her forget all about arguing with him.

# CHAPTER SEVEN

Tabitha piped little roses on decadent pieces of chocolate with a shaky hand. The burst of cold that waved through the workroom when the front door opened had her cursing as she messed up yet another delicate flower.

Brie bounced into the room like Tigger on his tail. She hung up her coat, whistling a tune that Tabitha couldn't place. She draped her apron over her head and tied it around her waist, then turned to grin at Tabitha. "I knew you'd be in here working too early."

"Early? It's seven. I'm always here by now."

"I know. You don't have a life." She headed for the sink to wash her hands. "If you did, you'd understand the joy of sleeping in."

"I do to have a life." She cursed again as she scraped yet another damaged flower from the chocolate.

"You're in a mood again." Brie waltzed through the room and stood in front of her studying her. "You had a fight with Preston."

"No, I did not." She piped another flower, and though not perfect, she was going to let it slide.

"You didn't fight with him, but your hair is an absolute mess, you don't even have on your obligatory mascara, and you're scowling."

Tabitha shot her head up and glared at her, but instead of getting to work like Tabitha had hoped, the grin on Brie's face widened and she grabbed Tabitha's hands, shooting red frosting from the tube to the table.

"Oh, my God, you got laid!"

"Stop it." Tabitha snapped back her hands. "Get to work."

"I want details. I want lots of details."

"You're not getting any. I don't want to talk to you." She went back to piping flowers.

But Brie didn't go anywhere. She pulled a stool up to the table and perched herself on top of it. Setting her elbows on the table, she rested her face in her hands and stared at Tabitha with her annoying grin plastered on her lips. "So how was it? How was he? I can't believe you slept with him." She reached across the table and gripped Tabitha's hands again. "I can't believe you finally got laid."

"I thought that was how men talked." Preston's voice boomed through the shop from the doorway. He stood there with a tray of coffee and a brown bag in his hands. "You're kissing and telling?" Tabitha hated that he looked so sexy with that grin on his lips, especially when all she wanted to do was punch him for playing into Brie's asinine gossip.

As soon as Brie saw him, she squealed and jumped down from her stool. She ran to him and enveloped him in a huge hug, forcing him to balance the tray of coffees, and then placed a big, noisy kiss on his cheek.

"You got her. You got her!"

Preston chuckled. "I got her."

"Are you two thirteen?" Tabitha threw down the tube of frosting. "This isn't open for discussion."

Brie stomped her feet in a little dance. "It should be. I'm dying for some deets."

"Deets?"

"Details." Brie bounced back to her stool and sat down. She shifted her eyes between Tabitha and Preston. "So, who's going to tell me. Was it good?"

Preston walked toward Tabitha and handed her a coffee. He took a moment to gaze into her eyes and then placed a soft kiss on her lips. No matter how mad she was at that moment, she felt it slip away as he lingered his lips on hers.

He glanced at Brie. "It was fucking awesome." He smiled then gave Tabitha's butt a swat.

That was all it took to make the anger pulse through her again. She pushed her hands into his chest, and he stumbled back and out of her way. Tabitha took her coffee and huffed off to her office. She slammed the door and then kicked it hard enough she was sure she'd broken a toe.

Tabitha hopped over to the chair that faced her desk, her hot coffee wobbling in her hand. She set it on the desk and then fell into the chair. Her foot ached now. Temper sizzled in her veins, and embarrassment washed over her.

Why was she so put off by being in love and having had great sex with a man? Brie was forever giving her *deets* about her encounters and, sadly, Tabitha had listened intently to all of her tales. Even her own mother had come into the store on more than one occasion and shared details of evenings with men, which was a little too much for Tabitha to handle, but she'd done it.

So why couldn't she tell her best friend that she'd had the most amazing night with Preston? That he'd touched her in all the right places and melted her with kisses. Why was it a shameful secret that they'd had sex no less than five times and she'd only had three hours sleep. The man had taken off work to come into the store and help her put out her orders, when in one day he could make more than she'd make in a month.

It was love and she knew that, but she couldn't even embrace what was going on around her and enjoy it. No, now she sat in her office with a broken toe, red fingers from spilled icing, and an attitude as bad as her hairdo.

She hated that she couldn't even enjoy the moment even though that was all she wanted to do. She wanted to embrace love. She wanted to be giddy and tell her best friend all the deets. She wanted to run out into that other room, kiss Preston Banks until he ran out of breath, and then tell him she'd marry him in some spur of the moment wedding.

Instead, she hobbled around to the other side of her desk and began to call her vendors for the supplies she'd need delivered.

Tabitha made her last phone call and sat quietly at her desk. She could hear the radio in the other room playing and muffled voices beyond the door. She glanced at the clock and realized she'd been holed up in her office all morning. The rumbling in her stomach alerted her that it was lunchtime, and she'd never eaten the pastry Preston had brought with the coffee.

It was time to stop hiding and face the music. She'd had sex with Preston Banks and now Brie knew all about it. Big deal, she thought as she readjusted the ponytail at the back of her head.

Tabitha hobbled to the door, now sure that she'd only bruised her foot and not broken her toe. Slowly, she opened the door and stood amazed that the only person in the room was Brie.

"You're alone?"

"Yes, well, this is my job." Brie boxed up chocolates in a printed, white box and set them in the stack to be sealed.

"I mean, I heard voices. Where is Preston?"

"He has a life, you know." She was being short with her and Tabitha didn't like it, but she was in no position to argue otherwise.

"Are you hungry?"

Brie put a lid on the box she'd just filled with an assortment of chocolates and turned to glare at her. "I'm starving. I'll fly if you buy."

Tabitha replaced the frown that was hurting her face with an evenly forced smile. "I'll fly and buy, if you don't mind. I need a few moments out."

Brie nodded. "I hear there's a great pizza joint not too far from here."

Tabitha clenched her jaw and balled her hands into fists at her side. "So, is that what's been going on out here? You got all the gossip you wanted?"

"Whoa!" Brie held up her hands and laughed. "Paranoid. No, he didn't give away any gossip. In fact, he was quite concerned that you never came out of your office. Furthermore, the only information I got out of him was that he took you for pizza the other night. Hence, the reason I'm hungry for it now. Is that all okay with you?"

"He was concerned about me?"

"That's what happens when people fall in love, Tabitha." She turned back to her assembly of candy boxes. "Not that you've gone and done that at all. Or, at least, not that you'll tell me. I want pepperoni by the way and a big soda."

Tabitha grabbed her coat and purse from the hook and left the store.

When Tabitha walked through the door of the restaurant, where she'd dined with Preston only a few days earlier, she groaned. There was a line seven people deep. This was why she didn't leave the store during lunchtime. But she, at least, owed Brie lunch for being so snippy to her all morning.

She stepped up into the line and nearly screamed as someone in the booth to her right reached out and grabbed her hand.

"I have a seat for you all ready if you'd consider joining me."

Preston looked up at her with those dark eyes and his sexy grin. She noticed there was a pizza on the table, two drinks, and an empty plate next to him.

"You knew I was coming here?"

He cocked his head to the side. "Brie likes to plan things out."

Tabitha blew out a hard breath. "Yes she does, but this is none of her business."

Preston stood from the booth and guided her to it. She slid in, and he did the same sitting right next to her as if to block her in and keep her from escaping. He took a slice of pizza from the tray and put it on her plate. Then he filled her cup with soda from the pitcher which sat on the table. "Eat."

Tabitha sat still for another moment with her hands in her lap, clenched into fists. "Why are you doing this?"

"Eating pizza? Because Brie mentioned it and it made me hungry."

"Why are you even still talking to me? I was childish back at the store. I shouldn't worry about what other people think about what I do in the privacy of my own home, but I lashed out at you and my best friend." She turned her head to look him in the eye. "Why do you want to be with me?"

Preston lifted his pizza slice to his mouth, took a bite, and considered her as he chewed. "I think you have it all figured out already."

"I don't have anything figured out. I'm a wreck." She looked at the pizza, but didn't pick it up yet. She just wasn't ready to taste food when the vile taste of shame was thick on her tongue.

"You're so caught up in not letting anyone near you, you're trying to push us all away. The only person who seems to be able to whittle away at you is my mother. In case you haven't noticed, she's a little invasive."

"She is not." She finally picked up the pizza slice and just held it. "I envy her. She's so confident."

"So are you. You just keep making excuses to not let others see it."

Tabitha set the slice back on the plate. "I thought you were trying to be nice to me."

"I am being nice to you. I bought you pizza. By the way, save a slice for Brie. I have to take some back with us." He bit into his slice. He swallowed his bite and washed it down with soda. "Let go. You don't have to be a hard ass because you think you have to protect yourself from living like your mother, who, by the way, is very happy."

"Love should be one time, not many."

"Says who?"

"Says me. Don't you believe in forever?"

"Yes, but I'm not one to deny those who keep diving in trying to find it either."

She opened her mouth to argue and then shut it and sunk into the booth. Was that what her mother was doing? She was testing the waters? Did her mother think forever was there and was so willing to gamble to find it that she took chances with her heart every chance she got? Then, there was Tabitha who didn't gamble at all and was miserable waiting for it.

A young bus boy walked past the table, and Preston asked for a box and a large soda cup. The boy returned with the box and cup, and Preston began to put the rest of the pizza in it while Tabitha sat silently thinking about what he'd said.

"If you're not going to eat that now, take it back with you. Don't waste it," he said, closing the box and filling the cup with the rest of the soda in the pitcher.

It hit her all at once. And she realized, as she watched Preston box up the pizza, that she had indeed wasted it – her life.

Love was something to chase, to seek, to find. Why had she sat by and created masterpieces for others to give to someone they loved and not taken even a moment to try to find love herself?

This was it. Love was in her grasp and it didn't come with guarantees and planning. It came fast and hard. It knocked you off balance and made you lightheaded. That, she realized, was part of the charm.

Preston closed the box and settled a look on her that sent her blood pressure rising. She wasn't going to waste happiness and the opportunity given to her by a man who was willing to risk everything just to be with her. "I won't waste it," she said looking at him. When his eyes locked onto hers, she knew he understood. She wasn't talking about the pizza any longer.

"That's a big decision."

Tabitha pressed her hand to her pounding heart. "I'm scared to death."

Preston turned to face her completely. "I'm not a runner. I don't give up very easily."

"I know."

"Don't think that, if you change your mind tomorrow, I'll just tuck my tail between my legs and walk away." She nodded and he gave her a careful scan with his eyes. "I fight for what I believe in. And I believe in forever, love at first sight, quick romances, and you."

Tabitha sucked in a breath and blew it back out slowly. "God, you've just scared me again."

"Good, then you'll think about it even harder."

"I don't want to think anymore. Thinking holds me back, always has."

"I won't argue that." He moved in closer. "I'm staying at your place tonight. And tomorrow."

Tabitha bit down on her lip and nodded.

"Then I have weddings to run on Friday and Saturday, and you're going with me."

"Okay."

"We're staying at my place those nights."

Again, she nodded and let her shoulders relax.

"Next week is Valentine's week. I already have the week off to help Mom with the weddings she has planned. I'm going to help you with your orders. Then I am going to be your date to your mother's wedding."

She felt the blood drain from her face. Her mother's wedding. She'd nearly let all the planning slide on it because she didn't want to think about it. "My mother. I need to get to her and help her with the wedding."

Preston smiled wide. "Well, now I think you're truly making a recovery from being a hard ass about all this love stuff."

The shop was bustling when Tabitha and Preston walked through the door. Brie was calling out orders to those in the back while she helped customers at the counter.

"Glad you're back. We've had a rush." She handed Tabitha a box and a ribbon. "Tie this while I ring it up." She looked at Preston. "Go on back. Your mom is in charge of the prep area. She'll tell you where to go."

"Yes, ma'am." He handed Brie the box of pizza and the soda cup then slipped away though the doorway.

Brie punched in the prices into the cash register and gave the customer their total. "If you don't keep him, I'll take him," she said with her head tilted toward Tabitha while she waited for the customer to hand her the money for the sale.

"He's spoken for," she said without looking up.

The customer handed her the money and Brie stopped. "You mean it?"

Tabitha finished the knot with the ribbon and reached behind her for a bag. She carefully slid the box of chocolates inside the bag and handed it to the customer as Brie hastily handed him his change and then quickly turned her attention back to Tabitha.

When she'd steadied her nerves, Tabitha took a deep breath and faced her best friend. "I mean it."

Brie gripped her arms and watched her closely. "I never thought I'd see the day you fell in love."

"Don't make a big deal." She tried to turn away, but Brie kept her pinned.

"It is a big deal. You're in love. You love him." She shook her head slowly. "I can see it in your eyes. This one is it. He's your forever."

Tabitha swallowed the lump that had formed in her throat. "Stop. I think I'm doing fairly well just giving in. Don't make me freak out."

"Oh, you'll freak out all right. You'll lose your mind over it. That's how you are. But this time, at the end of the day, he'll be there." Brie pulled her tightly to her and squeezed until Tabitha thought she'd crush a rib. "I'm so happy for you."

"Okay. Okay." She pushed back. "Let's just keep it low. I need to get through next week and my mom's wedding, and then I can see what happens."

Brie turned around to the display case and arranged the chocolates on the trays. "I think you should go away with him." She turned her head to look at Tabitha. "After the fifteenth, of course."

"Of course. And where would we go?"

"Anywhere. Hawaii. Las Vegas. Vail and hide away in a cabin surrounded by snow."

Tabitha was sure she'd seen Brie's eyes glaze over. "I have to get back to work. My mother is going to need my level head this week. I sure hope I can give that to her."

# CHAPTER EIGHT

Guilt was a great motivator. Tabitha had promised her mother to help her with her wedding, not just the chocolates. However, when she sat down at her mother's table a mere six days before the wedding, she realized she hadn't helped at all.

She hadn't helped address the invitations, she only helped drop them in the mail. Peter had taken her mother to the dress store to pick out her dress, not her. The flowers, oh, she'd helped with that. She'd called an acquaintance and told her, "Whatever you have left over will do."

Tabitha was sick to her stomach. "I've really let you down." She looked down at the guest list, which was much bigger than she'd remembered - or expected.

"You've never let me down." Her mother reached across the table and gave Tabitha's hand a squeeze. "You're quite a woman. I'm proud of who you are."

"I should have helped you more. I've been so defiant about all of this." She waved her arm over the mound of papers and receipts that lay in front of them.

"It wasn't fair of me to ask you to do so much. I understood that early on. You have a very successful business and this time of year I should be helping you, not asking you to do the one thing you despise the most."

Tabitha pursed her lips. "And what is it I despise the most?"

"Weddings. People falling in love and getting all ooey-gooey over each other." Even the words made Tabitha tense, but this time not because they disgusted her, but because she knew the real power in them.

"I still should have had some consideration for your feelings, and Peter's."

"I know you love me. And I know I have caused you so much pain by being so free with falling in love. But, Tabby, I can't help it. Love is so wonderful and I want to hold it for as long as it will last." She threw her hands in the air. "Oh, I'm a sucker for chocolates and flowers. I never tire of hearing the words I love you. Falling asleep in the arms of the man you love is priceless."

"But do you even know if it's real anymore?" Tabitha didn't like the way it sounded, but her mother was still smiling when she leaned in over the table.

"It's all real, Tab. All of it." She patted her hand again and stood. She walked to the cupboard and took down two wine glasses. "Sure, I haven't been very lucky when it comes to longevity, but I've never been sad."

Tabitha thought about it. No matter what state of love she was in, whether it was the falling in or falling out of, her mother was happy. As if she knew the end wasn't forever.

She watched as her mother opened a bottle of wine and filled the two glasses.

Oh, she'd shed her share of tears and so had Tabitha. Each man who came in and out of their lives over the years was almost equally important to Tabitha as they'd been to her mother, only Tabitha hadn't taken their leaving as well as her mother had.

Her mother set the glasses on the table and sat back down across from Tabitha. She took the invitations and began to sort through them. "This is going to be a beautiful wedding."

"Mom, do you think this is the one? The one forever."

Her mother smiled and lifted her glass to her lips. "I hope so."

It wasn't yes. It wasn't no. Yet her mother sat before her with glazed over eyes and a smile that would light the room.

Tabitha felt a jolt in her stomach. She didn't know if it was fear or the universal understanding that love was to be enjoyed in the moment and worked on forever. She was so worried about getting beyond the end that she'd never let there be a beginning.

She began to gather the papers that lay before her. "It looks like everything is in order. I'll confirm the flowers." And see if she could make the floral arrangements something better than what was left over. "I'll check on the hall and the caterer."

"Thank you, Tabitha."

She stood and gathered her purse and her coat from the back of the chair. "I hope its okay that I'd like to bring Preston with me."

"Oh, darling, it's more than okay." Her mother stood. "The two of you seem to be getting pretty serious."

Tabitha let out a steady breath. "I'm learning what that means. My practical way of thinking says it's much too early to talk about being serious."

"And you're unpractical?"

Tabitha felt her cheeks rise as she smiled at her mother. "My unpractical says I should enjoy this moment because I think I've fallen in love with him."

Her mother's wide grin must have surpassed even her own. "Do enjoy it."

Tabitha slipped on her coat and pulled on her gloves. Her mother kissed her on the cheek as she left the house and headed out into the bitter winter in Colorado, but, for the first time, she didn't feel the cold. Her body resonated warmth from the inside.

Tabitha pulled up outside of her house and the warmth that had filtered through her only increased when she saw Preston's car parked out front.

He opened his door and stepped out into the street as Tabitha parked her car. "I wondered if you'd forgotten our arrangement."

His heavy, leather coat was zipped to the neck and sleek leather gloves covered his hands, but she wondered if he could even feel the cold. She hadn't felt it all day.

With the door to her car still open, she ran to him. She barreled her body into his, knocking him slightly off balance. Her arms encircled his neck and his hands gripped her hips. When she pressed her lips to his she felt the cold chill that had settled on them, but a moment later the warmth from her mouth made his pliant.

Her fingers tunneled through his hair and her tongue sought out to tempt his senses. Tabitha pressed harder to him and he wrapped his arms around her.

When her breath was gone, she pulled back slightly from the kiss to take in the view of him. His dark hair had channels from where she'd run her fingers. His lips were soft from the warmth of her kiss, and his eyes were just a bit hazy.

He pulled her in tighter. "That took me a bit by surprise."

"I missed you."

He pushed her back at arm's length and looked her over from head to toe. "You did?"

Tabitha nodded. "I couldn't get home to you quick enough." She pushed up to him again. "Let's get inside. I'm not done with you."

"I certainly can't argue with that logic."

She ran back to her car and slammed the door and then ran up the front stairs with Preston right behind her.

As soon as they shut the cold outside behind the door, there was a whirlwind of coats and gloves falling to the floor. Preston pressed Tabitha up against the wall and began the task of unbuttoning her shirt. She loosened the belt around his waist as their mouths ravaged hot against one another's.

When her shirt fell to the floor, his hands moved swiftly to her breasts. He peeled back the lace that covered them. He didn't unfasten her bra, he worked around it. When her skin was bare, he took each one into his hands and then into his mouth.

Tabitha's head fell back against the wall. The quick work she'd made unbuttoning his pants slowed drastically as he clamped his mouth around her swollen, sensitive nipple. Pleasure shot from her chest down between her legs.

She dragged her fingers through his hair again and gave a little tug. "We have to get to the bedroom."

"No. Here. Now." His voice was low and growled out his desires in a caveman's grunt. He pulled her away from the wall and lowered her onto the cold tile beneath them.

Tabitha arched her skin away from the cold on her back as Preston pulled off her shoes and sent them flying into the other room. A moment later, he was giving her jeans a hard yank and ripping them from her legs. His mouth quickly went back to work over her stomach and back up to her breasts.

She reached around him and slid her hands down the back of his pants. His firm butt was like putty in her hands that she molded. Her hands still in his pants, she began to push them away as he kicked off his shoes. Preston adjusted so he could push away the constrictive clothing then returned to her.

"Damn," he growled as he reached behind them and reeled in his pants to pull his wallet from the pocket. He unloaded the contents until he found the foil packet then ripped it open with his teeth.

She watched as he hurried to roll on the condom and was almost willing to risk it all to move on and have him inside of her. But he finished quickly and slid inside of her which forced her to lie back on the hard, cold floor with the onslaught of pleasure. Within a moment, she forgot about the discomfort under her as the weight and heat of her lover moved over her, in her.

The pace was quick and urgent. Fingers clawed at flesh. Teeth nipped at tender spaces. Moans rattled in her chest and only half of them were hers.

Every muscle in her body tightened and, as they did, his body pressed closer and closer to hers. He gripped her hips as she pulled her legs around him tighter.

Any composure she had left liquefied as she pulsed around him and he released. His body was heavy on hers as he caught his breath and regained his strength.

"That warmed me up." His voice was low in her ear.

"You're not the one with your back on the tile."

"Nope, I'm the one with my knees on it." He groaned a laugh into her neck and she held him tight.

Never had she thought she'd embrace a man on a cold, tile floor and wonder if it was necessary to let him go – ever.

The glow from the television flickered in the dark room. Tabitha laid perfectly still in Preston's arms. A thin sheet wrapped around them, their limbs entangled, and he slept while she thought.

It was a harsh reality when you were thirty, had been in a couple relationships, and suddenly realized not once had you ever been in love. Never in her life had she been as comfortable in a man's arms as she was in Preston's. However, her mother's track record made her leery of the happiness she was feeling. When would it end? When would they grow tired of each other?

He shifted around her. "You should be sleeping," he said. His voice was low and gruff with sleep.

When she shifted to look at him, his eyes were closed. She let out a sigh. "I can't."

"Turn off the TV then." He pressed his face into the crevice of her neck and placed small, soft, warm kisses on her skin. "I could give it another go. Try and wear you out a little more."

Tabitha chuckled and searched the bed around her for the remote to the TV. She turned it off and the room grew completely dark.

"I'm completely worn out and have to be at work in a few hours." She rolled up next to him until her naked body pressed against his. "But I'm willing to let you try."

He let out a moan that bordered on tired and aroused. Tabitha wrapped her arms around his neck as he gripped her hip in his hand, but the advancement stopped there as he peeled open his sleepy eyes and stared at her.

The feel of his body next to her, and his obvious arousal, should have been reason enough for her smile. Instead, it was the sincerity of his look as he locked his gaze into her eyes.

"I love you," he said. His voice was low, but steady.

Her urge was to back away, but his hands held her in place and his eyes held her to an answer. She sucked in the air necessary to make the commitment. She willed her rapid heart rate to still. But when his lips curled into a sleepy smile she lost the control she fought for. "Preston, I love you too."

Tabitha was happy to have had two hours alone in her store. The music blared and chocolates were plentiful this morning.

She danced around her workspace and her cheeks hurt from smiling, but she knew it was all going to have to end before Brie got there or she'd never hear the end of it.

Too late. Tabitha looked up and nearly screamed aloud when she saw Brie standing in the doorway with her mouth wide open.

Tabitha let out a loud *humph*, wrinkled up her nose and hurried to the radio to turn it down. With her hand still on the volume control, she watched as her best friend shook her head in disbelief. "I don't know if I should kiss you or kick you."

"Neither please." Tabitha's smiled again. "We're almost caught up."

"That's because you're not grumping around. See what love can do?" Brie walked in and hung her coat on the hook, yawned, and put on her apron. "I'm glad to see you're happy."

But Brie's voice wasn't happy. Her whole demeanor wasn't right. She should have been dancing in circles around the room with her, but she tied on her apron and went straight to the order wall. Didn't she want *deets*? Didn't she want to hear about them making love on the tile floor and then again in the bed?

This moment of friendship was being wasted. God, Tabitha thought she might explode. Is this how horrible a friend she'd been when she'd walked into a room and Brie was dancing around it? Had she, herself, merely grunted when Brie spoke of love and sex? Yes, that was exactly what she'd done. Karma was, in fact, a bitch. But there was something more. Something wasn't right. Tabitha didn't know how to approach it except head on.

She turned off the radio and walked to the prep table where Brie looked over the order she'd taken off the wall. "You okay?"

"Sure."

"Do you want to talk?" When Brie shifted her eyes to her, Tabitha knew she'd been crying and now was in even more unfamiliar territory.

"Do you? I usually get your mom for these talks."

The blow to her ego was strong, but she tried to let it pass without wincing.

Her mother was a good listener. Tabitha could admit that. And one of the reasons they were such good friends was that her mother had taken a liking to Brie as if she were a daughter. It didn't surprise her that Brie would think of talking to her mother before she'd talk to her, but it stung.

Tabitha touched her arm. "I'm here if you need an ear." She turned to walk back to her prep table.

"I'm pregnant." That stopped her forward progress and she took a moment before she turned around. "I was stunned into silence, too."

Tabitha took a few steps toward her. "Wow. I wasn't expecting that at all."

"Trust me. Neither was I." She blew a wayward curl from her eyes. "But this is my reality. I'm okay with it. It was just kind of a shock."

"Did you tell the father?"

"Greg?" Tabitha searched for the name, but she didn't recognize it and her face obviously registered the confusion. Brie's lips pursed. "Video guy."

"Oh, Greg. I thought his name was John."

"So did I. And he's married. He forgot to mention that, too."

Tabitha felt the sudden need to grip the table and steady herself. This was why fast love was so wrong. This was what happened to her mother, minus the already married part.

Her knees had gone soft, but she kept herself upright against the table. Love at first sight. Head over heels in love. Blinded by love. It was everything Tabitha hadn't believed in, and, now that she felt the giddy pleasure, here stood her best friend in the world burned by those very things.

She thought back to the night she'd had with Preston and the immense pleasure she'd had by letting go. But had she let go too much? They'd been careful, but how careful. If she didn't put a stop to it right away she'd end up like Brie with a baby and a broken heart. It was her childhood all over again. She could feel it forming around her.

Brie reached for her. "Are you okay?"

"Me? Yes, I'm fine."

"I'm the queasy one and you look like you're going to faint." Brie hurried around the table and pulled a stool to her. She sat down as Brie ran to the sink and wet a towel. She handed it to her and Tabitha placed it on her forehead. "You're sure you're okay?"

Tabitha nodded.

Brie laughing wasn't what she'd expected. "I catch you in here dancing and humming to loud music, tell you I'm pregnant, and now you're the one who is going to faint. I think you owe me some juicy gossip."

Tabitha looked at her in disbelief. Had Brie not heard herself? Brie's life was over as she knew it. The man she'd temporarily loved left her with a baby and a lie to live with. How could she just change gears and want gossip?

"Aren't you upset by all of this?" Tabitha asked, realizing her tone bordered on accusation.

"The baby? Hell, no. It happens all the time, Tab. Neither one of us would be here if it hadn't been for the fluke of luck our mother's had. Am I upset that he lied to me? Yeah. I'm pissed off like you wouldn't believe." Brie went back to studying the order she'd taken from the wall. "I had thought about calling his wife and telling her, but then realized it wouldn't do any good. She'd think I was some crazy woman and hang up on me. Besides, I'm fairly sure I can get him fired."

The room was quiet, but then Brie looked up at Tabitha and grinned and the hysterical laughter broke free.

Each of them tried to hold it in, tried to bury it under the severity of the situation. But it didn't work. Soon the laughter rolled from them, their stomachs hurt, and their cheeks ached.

But Tabitha stopped laughing when she looked up and Preston stood in the doorway with a tray of coffees for each of them and a pastry bag. He was the face of reality. The vivid reminder that she needed to end their relationship before it became a laughing matter to Brie.

Tabitha Knight didn't believe in love at first sight and quick relationships, and Brie's situation sealed that for her. She and Preston were over.

# CHAPTER NINE

Preston set the coffees on the table. "You girls seem to be having a lot of fun this morning."

"Nah," Brie walked over to the table and picked up one of the cups. "It's the hysterical laughter that comes after a tense situation."

Tabitha watched Preston's face shield in worry. He walked around Brie and straight to Tabitha, touching her shoulder. "Are you all right? Did something happen?"

Tabitha couldn't answer. She stood there staring at him, wondering what might be going through his mind.

"Oh, not her," Brie said with her mouth full from a pastry she'd taken from the bag. "Me. I got myself knocked up."

The lines in Preston's forehead softened and he turned away from Tabitha. "Congratulations?"

"I'll take it. The baby's daddy is an ass, but I'm happy. Who'd have thought I'd have a kid." She shrugged.

Tabitha's mouth fell open. How could she seriously be so nonchalant about it? She was talking about bringing a life into the world. Someday that life would wonder what she was thinking, too. A woman on her own, dumped by a casual sex partner, having to raise a child. And would she end up like Tabitha's mother? Would she marry every man she met trying to find that love that didn't even exist with the father of her own child?

"I have some paperwork to do," Tabitha said. She walked past Preston, picked up her coffee and pastry, and walked into her office nearly slamming the door behind her.

She set the coffee and pastry on her desk and paced back and forth. It shouldn't be about her, she knew that, but she couldn't help it. Brie's situation made hers that much worse.

The tapping on the door had Tabitha turning around. Preston stood there with the door open slightly. The mask of worry was back on his face and she didn't like the way it looked. He inched through the door slightly. "Do you want to talk?"

"No."

"Too bad." He stepped into the room and shut the door behind him. "What's going on?"

She moved behind her desk and sat down in her chair. Then she stood back up and paced again. "What's going on? Did you hear her? She's pregnant."

"Yes. She's going to name the boy Fred, after an uncle. That is, if it's a boy. But Fred?" His face had crinkled up again then softened into a smile before that, too, faded. "So, why are you all worked up over this?"

"Because this was my life. My mother had me and my father didn't love her."

"And your life sucks, right?"

"What? No. Well..." It did sound bad when he said it that way. Fury bubbled in her belly now and she wanted to tell him that she didn't like being talked down to. But, at the same time, she felt childish having such a fit, but it wasn't passing. "It just wasn't easy watching my mom go through all of that." She tensed her hands and then tried to relax them, but it did little to calm her.

"I know I haven't been around a long time, but it seems to me that Brie and your mother have a good relationship. Much of that is because they do understand each other. And, honey," he said as he stepped closer to the desk, "your mother is one terrific woman who loves you very much."

Tabitha sat down in her chair and planted her hands on the top of the desk. "I don't think you and I should see each other anymore."

His eyes shot open as if she'd punched him in the gut. Color moved into his cheeks, but the redness slowly faded as he took a few breaths. "You don't want to see me anymore because your best friend is pregnant?"

"Yes. No." She stood up again and the anger in her belly weighed her down like a Thanksgiving dinner. She hated the feeling, but it was the right thing to do. "Because it's too fast."

"That's how relationships work, Tabitha. You meet. You have chemistry. You fall in love." He inched even closer. "You told me you loved me."

Tabitha pushed back her shoulders and straightened her spine as if it would give her courage to face him. "I shouldn't have."

"You're right. Maybe you shouldn't have."

He was quick and was around the desk before she knew he'd taken a step. His hands gripped her arms and he yanked her against him. The warmth of his mouth crushed down on hers. It took her under hard, fast, and scrambled her mind.

His grip was still tight on her arms when he pushed back and looked at her. She caught her breath and tried her hardest to look stern, but she knew she was failing miserably.

"You have six hundred truffles to roll this morning for an order that I will pick up at eight in the morning for the wedding I'm working. You'd better get to work." He let go of her and walked back to the door. "I have been assigned to strawberry dipping duty because Brie says my mother does it so well. Do you have any objections?" She didn't say anything, she couldn't. "Good. When you get yourself together, we'll be out here waiting for you. My mom will be here later to help, too. She knows she buried you at a busy time. And Brie said your mother was coming too. Looks like you'll have to put on your happy face if you want to make this Valentine season work out for you."

He shut the door behind him, and she was alone in her office again with nothing but her thoughts. But this time she had an overwhelming case of guilt to have to deal with too.

It took Tabitha the better part of an hour to emerge from her office. By the time she did, the workroom was full of people, music, and conversation.

"Good morning, darling." Her mother looked up at her from a tray of truffles she rolled in cocoa. "Did you hear Brie's great news?" Tabitha nodded. "I told her we get the honor of the baby shower. Won't that be fun?"

Tabitha looked at Brie who smiled wide, and she realized that her reaction had been wrong and completely selfish. Brie was like her mother in so many ways. They welcomed opportunities, like babies and new love. Only Tabitha would be so shallow to have nearly thrown away the best relationship she'd ever had just because her best friend was pregnant and the video rental guy didn't care.

In an apologetic move, she walked to Brie and hugged her tightly. "I'm happy for you if this is what you really want."

"I'm happy, Tab." She pulled back to look at her. "It's going to be hard and scary, but I have all of you to support me when I think I can't do it. I'm not alone and my baby won't be either."

She was right. She'd never be alone.

The work in the room had slowed and Tabitha knew all eyes were on her. But when she turned and Preston's lips curled into a soft smile, she couldn't be mad any longer.

She ran across the room and straight to him. She wrapped her arms around his neck as he hoisted her around his waist. Her mouth was quick to take his as he staggered then regained his balance.

She rested her forehead against his. "I'm sorry."

"I knew you were when you were breaking up with me." He set her back on her feet. "I still love you, Tabitha. Nothing is going to change that."

She looked around the room. Her mother and her best friend had stopped working to listen. If she said what was in her heart they would both know she'd lost her mind. But if she didn't say what was there, she might lose the one man who ever did love her.

"I love you, Preston. That hasn't changed."

Tabitha couldn't have been more pleased with the progress of the day or the sales. The pace and the mood never slowed or diminished. Tabitha accepted orders that she wouldn't normally have taken so close to the holiday. Customers waited in a line that never ended. They ordered in pizza for lunch, since Brie now had a craving for it, and Tabitha suspected it would also be dinner as she and her volunteer crew kept working.

By the time the store closed late, Tabitha was exhausted, but she knew she could work another three hours because there were that many more orders.

Brie leaned against the wall. "Have we ever been so busy?"

"No. This will be our biggest February in history." There was lightness in her voice that she almost didn't recognize. It had been such a long time since she'd been so happy about so many things. She looked over at Brie, who had closed her eyes. "Why don't you go home?"

"There is still more to do," Brie argued as she yawned.

"Yes, and Preston is here to help me."

"You talked me into it then." Brie peeled herself from the wall. "I'll be back early in the morning."

Tabitha pulled a tray from the display case and boxed up the three candies that remained. "I tell you what. Why don't you come in about noon. I'm going with Preston to a wedding tomorrow night. You can close up. I can see if my mom will stay with you."

"I'll be fine." She disappeared into the back room and returned with her coat. "Can I take home some of that pizza? I'm starving again."

"You're going to gain seventy pounds."

"I plan on it. I want to." She pulled on her coat. "This is going to be great."

Tabitha watched Brie zip up her coat and walk out the door with the pizza box she'd already grabbed from the cooler.

"She's really happy, isn't she?" Preston's voice resonated from behind her.

She turned to see him standing against the same wall Brie had rested against a few minutes earlier. "I think she is happy. I think she's crazy, but happy." She pulled another tray from the display and removed the few candies that remained. "And I think she's going to milk it for everything."

"Any woman who carries a baby deserves to *milk* it."

"You mean that?" She turned to him, her hand on her hip. "She's going to gain seventy pounds she says."

"Isn't that the best part? Eat anything you want?"

"You don't think that's disgusting?"

"Um, no. I kinda think pregnant women are sexy." The apples of his cheeks were full and his eyes were soft when he mentioned it.

Tabitha laughed aloud and finished boxing up the chocolates in the display. "You're joking."

"No, I'm not." His voice was steady and serious. It caused her to turn and see that his eyes were focused on her and his face was now somber. "I think you would be extremely sexy pregnant."

She tore another box from the stack behind her and began to fill it. "I have no plans to be pregnant." When her finger broke through the delicate chocolate in her hand, she threw it to the floor and turned to him. "I have known you less than two weeks. And, in those two weeks, you have talked me into having dinner with you, and you have slept in my bed. We have had sex on my entryway tile floor, we have told each other we love each other, and now you're telling me I'd be sexy pregnant. I think you've lost your mind." She threw another chocolate into the box. "On second thought, I think I've lost mine."

Preston crossed his arms over his chest. "Are you finished recapping our relationship?" Tabitha huffed out a breath and put her hands on her hips. He shook his head and the softness in his eyes had given in to the darkness of anger. "I do love you and I don't need a lifetime of dating to know that. I know, in my heart, that you are the woman I want to marry and yes, I would love to have children with you."

She felt the blood drain from her face. She set down the box of chocolates and she backed against the counter for support.

Preston walked toward her and pinned her in with a hand on each side of her. "I'm not done telling you I love you. But you know, seeing that it makes you pale and nearly sick, I now see why no one has ever stuck around."

"Screw you."

"Screw you. Some of us want happiness. I happen to want it with you, and I know how much work that's going to be."

She planted her hands on his chest and pushed him back. "You make me sound like a sociology project." She paced the small area behind the counter then turned to him. "Can we take the girl who won't love and make her into a princess that will? I'm not interested."

"Don't be so full of yourself. You'll never be the princess type."

Her jaw dropped open, and Preston turned and walked into the workroom. Tabitha paced a few more steps and then followed his path to the other room.

"You have no idea what type I am."

"Sure I do. You're a hard ass."

"How dare you talk to me like that." She walked across the room and pulled the next order off the wall. "You can't peg a person in a week. Or two."

"I can peg a person in the first minute I meet them."

She snapped her head around and narrowed her gaze on him. "And what did you peg me for?"

"A hard ass."

"Why don't you just go home?" She turned back to the order.

He moved swiftly across the room and stood right next to her. "Because you and I had a deal. I sleep at your house tonight, and tomorrow you are my escort to the wedding and you stay at my house."

"I don't want to anymore."

"Too bad. We had a deal."

She took a step away from him. "I'm not some luxury car sale. You can't test drive me to see if I fit."

"Isn't that what you're doing to me? You're testing me to see when I'm going to run away. How far can I push him until he's just like all the men who have come in and out of my life?" He took a step back. "Trust me, I feel like I'm the one being test driven and you are a lead-footed driver."

Her shoulders rolled forward and she dipped her head. "I am testing you." She felt the burning of tears in her throat. "You failed miserably, by the way." The first tears fell from her eyes. "Any other man would have headed for the door after I was so rude to them when they were trying to buy their mother a box of candy.

"I thought you were charming."

She wiped away at the dampness on her cheeks. "I don't want to love you."

"It's easier for you to not think about forever, isn't it?" She nodded and he moved in closer. "Forever isn't what's scary. It's never that is scary. I *want* to love you forever. I *never* want to be without you."

His hand slid around her waist, and she turned into his arms and rested her head against his broad chest. "I don't know what to do."

"You keep making progress in knowing I'm not leaving. I'll be here forever if you'll have me."

"I want you."

He slipped his finger under her chin and lifted her face. "Then stop trying so hard to hate me."

He lowered his face and then his lips tenderly pressed against hers as she sucked back the last of her sobs. Preston pulled her closer to him. Her mind began to settle around the idea that she did love this man who held her so tightly. There was no reason to push him away again. Happiness was all around them. She deserved to enjoy it herself, and so did Preston.

With his mouth on hers and her body pliant to his touch, she knew they weren't going to escape the store without ravaging each other first.

# CHAPTER TEN

Tabitha gripped hold of the worktable as Preston's mouth moved against hers with a quickness which she knew would have her on her back right there in the workroom. As he pressed her against the table, her hand hit the bowl which she'd been using to make frosting.

Preston's lips left hers as he looked to see her hand covered in milk chocolate. He grabbed hold of her wrist, his body still pressed hard against hers, and lifted it to his mouth. His tongue made long lines on her palm as he licked the chocolate from her hand.

She'd never had a man kiss, or lick, the inside of her hand. It shot tingles up her arm and they filtered down through her whole body. Then his lips were back on hers and the sweet taste of chocolate was on his tongue. But when she felt his finger on her throat and the dripping sensation of liquid, she jerked back to see him painting her skin with chocolate.

Her jaw quivered as he traced that same line he'd drawn with his finger with his tongue. "You're good enough to eat." His voice was as low as the moan that resonated from her throat.

She reached beside her and dipped her finger into the chocolate as well. Tabitha pulled back from his mouth and traced his lips with the chocolate. Slowly, methodically, she used her tongue in quick movements, removing the tantalizing taste from him.

With every flick of her tongue, his body tensed against hers and his breath quickened. His hands gripped her hips and his fingers clawed into her skin. There wasn't time for soft and slow. She engulfed his chocolate lips with her own. The swirl of chocolate danced on her tongue and she could taste it on his, making his candy kiss even sweeter.

Preston pulled her away from the table, his fingers still gripping her waist, and, with their mouths still in a mad dance, he backed her through the workroom to her office where he kicked the door closed behind them.

Tabitha let out a laugh as he moved her to the desk, his mouth still hungry against hers. "No one is here. You didn't have to close the door."

His hands moved to the tie on her apron. "I assume Brie has a key."

"Yep. Glad you closed the door." His hands were on the button of her pants as she unfastened his belt.

Their mouths continued in a battle for breath, taste, and passion that drove them both nearly mad with anticipation. As soon as Tabitha had unbuttoned his pants, Preston kicked them to the floor and she did the same.

Both of them, half-dressed pressed against each other. Tabitha sat back on the desk as, once again, Preston reached for a condom in his wallet.

Tabitha's breath was rapid, but he wasn't coming to her. He was still fumbling with his wallet. "Hurry."

"We used them all." He turned back to her. "I'm going to have to carry a box."

The disappointment pumped through her veins as quickly as the heat from his kisses had. It shouldn't matter. She could just throw the caution to the wind.

He must have known what she was thinking when she looked back up at him and he shook his head. "Not after today. I know your reaction wouldn't be as accepting as Brie's." He handed her back her pants from the floor and pulled his to his waist. "When we get home," he said as he reached his hand to her cheek. "I'll make love to you until you can't stay awake."

She managed a smile.

He was admirable, to say the least. A gentleman in the truest form of the word. Hadn't she waited her whole life for a man like that? A man who knew when to pull back? A man who knew when to stay. He wasn't afraid of her. He wasn't afraid of quick romances and long relationship.

She looked at him as he buckled his belt and turned to open the door. She quickly jumped to her feet, found her pants, and pulled them on. As he stepped out the door, she made a move toward him. "Preston." Her voice teetered on the edge of panic and he turned. "Marry me."

"What?"

"Marry me."

His mouth, smeared in chocolate, slowly turned up at the edges and then his smile grew wider. "Did I hit your head on the desk?"

"Don't make fun of me." She was desperate. She needed him to take her seriously before she came to her senses and realized just what she was saying. "Marry me."

His smile faded and a crease formed between his eyebrows. "You're not kidding."

"No. I'm always serious, but I've never been more serious than I am at this very moment."

He reached for her hands and laced their fingers together. Dried chocolate crumbled to the floor. "Tabitha, this is a very serious matter. One I would have over done for you if I thought you'd been thinking about it."

"I'm not thinking. Don't you understand?" She wasn't sure she did either. "I'm afraid of flowers and words. I don't want promises that are empty. I want the real thing." She squeezed her fingers around his. "I'm not about wedding dresses and huge engagement rings. They scare me. I see people all the time get caught up in the planning, and they forget what it's all about." He only looked at her with a glazed over stare. "Preston, say you'll marry me."

He didn't answer. He stood there with his mouth open.

The silence was like a knife in her chest.

Finally, he took a breath and a step back. "Tabitha, I do believe in it all. But this wasn't how I wanted it."

The air whooshed from her lungs, and he let go of her hands and turned from her. She watched as he wiped his hands on a towel at a worktable, took his coat from the rack, and walked out of her store.

She hadn't moved in an hour. She was still perched on her desk, covered in dried chocolate, when Brie burst through the front door of the store at ten o'clock that night with a duffle bag over her shoulder.

"Are you okay?" She ran into the office and enveloped her into her arms.

Tabitha sobbed. The taste of chocolate was bitter on her tongue. "No. I asked him to marry me and he ran out."

"It's okay." Brie helped her to one of the chairs and then set the bag down next to her. "He called and said you were upset so I raced over."

"He's gone."

"No. He just needed time to think." Brie reached for the box of tissue from her desk and pulled one out. She dabbed Tabitha's eyes and wiped away the chocolate that was smeared on her face. "Listen, the bars are open for four more hours and, for the first time in your life, I'm your designated driver."

Through her tears Tabitha laughed. "I'm not going out."

"I'm not giving you a choice. I brought you a dress and some makeup, and I want to do this so please don't make me beg."

"I just want to go home and sulk."

"And you've drug my sorry ass out of this bakery for less so I'm doing it to you now. Paybacks, sister."

Brie opened the bag and unloaded its contents. She handed her the dress, and Tabitha shook her head. "It's February at night. I'm going to freeze my butt off in this." She held up the short dress with the thin straps. It was royal blue, and she thought Brie had worn it in her sister's wedding. "I can go in my jeans."

"Oh, no you can't. Do you want to sulk, or do you want to make him sorry?"

Couldn't she do both?

The next thing she knew, Brie was pulling the band from her hair and running a brush through her locks. The humor of the moment took over, and she began to laugh. Brie was right. There had been many times she'd ambushed her like this and, for the first time, she needed it.

By eleven o'clock, Tabitha looked like she was going to prom, but Brie was smiling widely. "Let's hit the town."

Tabitha had locked up and met Brie out front. Thank goodness she'd taken the time to warm up the car. The dress was ridiculous, and how did Brie walk in heels like the ones she'd brought Tabitha to wear? Oh, she was going to impress the masses when she fell on her face the moment she walked into the bar, Tabitha thought.

"You look better all cleaned up and not smeared in chocolate." Brie shook her head at Tabitha. "If I'd have known better, I'd think that fight started in the middle of something very fun."

Tabitha climbed in the car. "Shut up and drive." She shut the door and fastened her seatbelt. Slowly, she let out a breath. She still wasn't sure she wanted to hit the bar and forget about the night, but she owed it to Brie to try. After all, she hadn't been too kind to her either.

Brie hit the highway and headed out of town.

"Where are you going? We work less than a mile from at least six bars."

"More swanky. Trust me."

Brie exited the highway to Golden. But as she passed under the large welcoming arch, she passed another three bars. "Are we going to a frat party?"

"Now you're talking."

"Are you kidding me?" Leave it to Brie to be sitting next to her, pregnant by a man she didn't know, and now she wanted to party with college boys. The woman had lost her mind. Well, it wasn't going to last long. They would be out of there the moment Tabitha fell off the shoes.

Brie parked the car just on the side of the Green Room center, and Tabitha winced at the memories of dancing with Preston there. Now, she was just being mean to bring her there, and, even worse, where was she going to make her walk to for this party? Who built a college town on such steep hills? Didn't they assume people would fall down them when they'd partied too much?

Brie hurried out of the car and up the steep walk. Tabitha scurried quickly behind Brie, trying not to fall, as she headed for the side door of the center. "Where are you going? This is closed."

"I have to pee. They always have someone here. The door has to be open. I really have to pee, the party can wait."

"You're going to get us arrested."

"And then he'll have to come and get you. C'mon, I can't hold it."

Tabitha looked around as if to make sure no one would catch them. Brie tugged on the door and it flew open. God, she was madder at Preston Banks than she had been when he walked away. Because of him, she was going to land in jail with her crazy friend, and business was much too busy to spend time in jail.

As the door closed behind her, she realized she didn't see Brie anywhere. The center was dark except for the lights coming from the Green Room.

Tabitha stood for a moment longer, but Brie didn't emerge from wherever she had disappeared to.

Curiosity got the better of Tabitha as she inched her way through the building toward the room. It was her favorite place of all. Even if her last memory there was of Preston, it could still be her favorite.

She looked around again and saw that no one had seen her. She opened the door and looked in. There at her feet were the grand stairs that led to the dance floor. Thoughts of her mother walking down those stairs filled her with happiness. How lucky her mother had been to love so many times. Tabitha now understood that.

A man emerged from the shadows and walked onto the dance floor. Tabitha took a step back before she realized the man was Preston.

She looked behind her, and there was Brie grinning widely.

Preston walked up the steps to the landing below her and held out his hand to her. Again, she exchanged a glance with Brie as her hands began to shake and the heels under her feet began to wobble.

Brie nudged her slightly. "Go. He's waiting for you."

"You set me up," she whispered.

"Of course I did."

Tabitha held tightly to the rail and slowly took each of the nearly hundred steps toward the man who only a moment ago she hated. But now, here he stood in a suit in her favorite place, looking more amazing than he'd ever looked before.

She batted back the tears that stung her eyes. From the shadows, others emerged. Her mother and Peter. Claire Banks and her husband. There were others, and she assumed those were his brothers and sister.

Preston held out his hand to her when she reached him. "What's going on?"

"You asked me to marry you and that just wasn't right."

She nodded, and the first tear fell and was warm on her cheek.

Preston brushed it away and then knelt down on one knee in front of her. She lifted her fingers to her lips and tried to keep them from trembling, but it was no use.

"Tabitha Knight, I believe in tradition. I believe in love at first sight. I believe in falling madly in love with the first kiss. And I believe in the man proposing on one knee." He took her hand and kissed it gently. His eyes met hers, and she sucked in a breath as he smiled and his eyes shimmered in the dimly lit room. "Will you marry me? Right here. Right now in your favorite place with your favorite people surrounding us?"

The word was on the tip of her tongue, but she couldn't make a sound. All she could do was nod.

Preston stood and cupped her face in his hands. "I'll never leave. I'll never fall out of love with you. And I'll never stop wanting to give you candy kisses."

She felt the heat rise in her cheeks as she looked beyond him to their families, who stood looking up at them, and wondered if they understood his last statement.

Never in her wildest dreams would Tabitha ever have imagined that she'd be marrying a man after knowing him only two weeks. She looked at her mother whose smile was brilliant. Finally, Tabitha decided she was as happy in love as her mother had always been, and, looking back at Preston, she finally believed in happily ever after.

# ABOUT THE AUTHOR

Bernadette Marie grew up obsessed with pens and notebooks, each one filled with lists and ideas for stories. Not much has changed. This wife and mother of five sons has a passion for writing stories about falling in love, finding love where you left it, and strong families.

Bernadette Marie is an accomplished martial artist who holds a Black Belt in Tang Soo Do, and she is a chronic entrepreneur. She is a member of Romance Writers of America and Colorado Romance Writers.

Visit her website at www.bernadettemarie.com for news on upcoming releases, signings, appearances, and contests.